Happy (

A Well-c

You'll

Lots of love, Dee Viv Jen+Ben
x x x x
(+ Sandy).

LAMBERTO LAMBERTO LAMBERTO LAMBE
MBERTO LAMBERTO LAMBERTO LAMBER
ETO LAMBERTO LAMBERTO LAMBERTO LA
LAMBERTO LAMBERTO LAMBERTO LAMBE
RTO LAMBERTO LAMBERTO LAMBERTO LA
MBERTO LAMBERTO LAMBERTO LAMBE
ERTO LAMBERTO LAMBERTO LAMBERTO LA
LAMBERTO LAMBERTO LAMBERTO LAMBE
RTO LAMBERTO LAMBERTO LAMBERTO
LAMBERTO LAMBERTO LAMBERTO LA
TO LAMBERTO LAMBERTO LAMBERTO
MBERTO LAMBERTO LAMBERTO LAMBE
BERTO LAMBERTO LAMBERTO LAMBEE
LAMBERTO LAMBERTO LAMBE
TO LAMBERTO LAMBERTO LAMBERTO LAMB
TO LAMBERTO LAMBERTO LAMBERTO
BERTO LAMBERTO LAMBERTO LAMB
RTO LAMBERTO LAMBERTO LAMBERTO
LAMBERTO LAMBERTO LAMBERTO LAN
TO LAMBERTO LAMBERTO LAMBERTO LAMBERT
E LAMBERTO LAMBERTO LAMBER
BERTO LAMBERTO LAMBERTO LAMBERTO
TO LAMBERTO LAMBERTO LAMBERTO LAM
ETE LAMBERTO LAMBERTO LAMBERTO LAMBERTO L
RTO LAMBERTO LAMBERTO LAMBERTO L
TO LAMBERTO LAMBERTO LAME
MBERTO LAMBERTO LAMBERTO LAMB
ERTO LAMBERTO LAMBERTO LAMBERT
LAMBERTO LAMBERTO LAMBERTO L
ERTO LAMBERTO LAMBERTO
TO LAMBERTO LAMBERTO LAMBERTO LA
E LAMBERTO LAMBERTO LAMBERT
BERTO LAMBERTO LAMBERTO LAMB
ERTO LAMBERTO LAMBERTO LAMBERTO LAMBERTO LAMA
RTO LAMBERTO LAMBERTO LAMBERT
LAMBERTO LAMBERTO LAMBERTO LAMB

LAMBERTO LAMBERTO LAMBERTO

GIANNI RODARI

ILLUSTRATED BY
FEDERICO MAGGIONI

TRANSLATED BY
ANTONY SHUGAAR

MELVILLE HOUSE

BROOKLYN, NEW YORK

LAMBERTO LAMBERTO LAMBERTO

Originally published in Italian as *C'era due volte il barone Lamberto*

© 1980 Maria Ferretti Rodari and Paola Rodari, Italy
© 1991 Edizioni EL S.r.l., Trieste, Italy

Translation © 2011 Antony Shugaar
Illustrations by Federico Maggioni © Edizioni EL

First Melville House printing: October 2011

Melville House Publishing
145 Plymouth Street
Brooklyn, NY 11201
www.mhpbooks.com

ISBN: 978-1-935554-61-5

Printed in the United States of America

1 2 3 4 5 6 7 8 9 10

Library of Congress Cataloging-in-Publication Data

Rodari, Gianni.
 [C'era due volte il barone Lamberto. English]
 Lamberto Lamberto Lamberto / Gianni Rodari ; translated by Antony
Shugaar.
    p. cm.
 ISBN 978-1-935554-61-5
 I. Shugaar, Antony. II. Title.
 PQ4878.O313C4713 2011
 853'.914--dc23
                        2011026359

CHAPTER 1

IN THE MIDDLE OF THE MOUNTAINS LIES Lake Orta. In the middle of Lake Orta, though not exactly in the middle, is the island of San Giulio. On the island of San Giulio stands the villa of Baron Lamberto, an exceedingly elderly gentleman (he is ninety-three years old) who is very wealthy (he owns twenty-four banks in Italy, Switzerland, Hong Kong, Singapore, and so on) and invariably ill. He has twenty-four maladies. Only his butler Anselmo can remember them all.

Anselmo keeps a list of the illnesses, in alphabetical order, in a little pocket notebook: arteriosclerosis, arthritis, arthrosis, asthma, chronic bronchitis, and so forth all the way up to the Z's, with Zellweger Syndrome. Alongside each illness, Anselmo has written down which medicines need to be taken, at what time of day or night, the foods that are permitted and those that are forbidden, the advice of the various physicians:

"Stay away from salt, which will drive up your blood pressure."

"Reduce your sugar intake, which does not sit well with diabetes."

"Avoid excitement, stairways, breezes and drafts, rainfall, sunshine, and the moonlight."

There are times when Baron Lamberto feels a slight nagging pain here or there, but he can't quite pinpoint which of his illnesses is responsible. He'll ask his butler:

"Anselmo, a shooting pain here and another one there?"

"Number six, Lord Lamberto: duodenitis."

Or else, he will ask: "Anselmo, that dizziness again. What could it be?"

"Number nine, Lord Lamberto: your liver. Though we cannot rule out a little mischief from number fifteen, your thyroid condition."

The baron gets his numbers mixed up sometimes.

"Anselmo, I am really suffering from twenty-three today."

"Your tonsils?"

"No, my pancreas."

"Begging your pardon, Lord Lamberto, but we have the pancreas listed as number eleven."

"Isn't number eleven gallbladder?"

"Gallbladder's seven, Lord Lamberto. Look for yourself."

"Well, it doesn't matter, Anselmo, it doesn't matter. What's the weather like?"

"Foggy, Lord Lamberto. Temperature's dropping. Snowfall all along the Alps."

Baron Lamberto also owns a mansion in Egypt, just a stone's throw from the pyramids. He has another mansion in California. And then he has one on the Costa Brava, one in Catalonia, and another on the Costa Smeralda, in Sardinia. He also has well-heated apartments in Rome, Zurich, and Copenhagen. In the winter, however, he generally goes to Egypt to bake his old bones in the bright sunlight, especially his longer bones, which are important for their marrow, the biological powerhouse that manufactures red globules and white globules.

And so, once again, they set off for Egypt. But they didn't stay long. In fact, during a walk along the banks of the Nile, they met an Egyptian fakir and stood absorbed in conversation for a bit. Directly after this meeting, Baron Lamberto and his manservant Anselmo took the first plane back to Italy, and hurried back to the seclusion of the villa on the island of San Giulio, to work on certain experiments. Time went by, and soon they were not alone. In the attic of the villa, now, there were six people who, day and night, droned the baron's name over and over:

"Lamberto, Lamberto, Lamberto . . ."
"Lamberto, Lamberto, Lamberto . . ."

The first to start was young Signorina Delfina, and then Signor Armando took over from her. As Signor Giacomini finished up, Signora Zanzi started. Then it was Signor Bergamini's turn, followed by Signora Merlo, and then it came around to Signorina Delfina again. They each did a one-hour shift; at night, two-hour shifts.

"Lamberto, Lamberto, Lamberto . . ."
"Lamberto, Lamberto, Lamberto . . ."

Occasionally Signorina Delfina can't help but laugh. As she's about to fall asleep, she wonders: "What a strange job! What is it good for? Are rich people crazy?"

The other five don't laugh and they don't wonder. They're well paid: in fact, they receive the same salary as the President of the Italian Republic, plus board, lodging, and unlimited hard candy. The hard candy is in case their throats get parched. So why should they think twice?

"Lamberto, Lamberto, Lamberto..."

What they don't know is that in every corner of the villa there are tiny hidden microphones to capture their chanting, wired to tiny and equally invisible hidden speakers scattered throughout the villa below. There's a speaker under the pillow in Baron Lamberto's bed, there's another in the grand piano in the ballroom. There are two in the master bathroom: one is incorporated in the handle of the hot water faucet, the other is in the cold water faucet. At any moment of the night or day, whether he is in the library or the wine cellar, in the dining room or the bathroom, Baron Lamberto can press a button and listen:

"Lamberto, Lamberto, Lamberto..."

At least once every half hour, the butler Anselmo also checks to make sure that upstairs, in the attic, work is proceeding without interruption, that the name is being pronounced accurately, that every syllable is being given its proper emphasis, and that the six workers are honestly earning their salaries and hard candy.

At first, the baron is less than fully satisfied.

"You have to admit, Anselmo," he complains, "you can't hear the capital L."

"Unfortunately, Your Lordship, there doesn't seem to be a way of pronouncing upper-case letters differently

from lower-case letters. Spoken Italian does have its shortcomings."

"I understand, but it's troubling, Anselmo. The 'L' that begins my name sounds no different from the 'l' that begins leech, lizard, and lollipop. It's dispiriting. I have to wonder how the great Napoleon was able to tolerate the fact that the very same 'N' that began his imperial first name shared the initial sound of namby-pamby, natter, and nosehair."

"Or nursery, nausea, and nictitation," added Anselmo.

"What is nictitation?"

"To open and shut one's eyes momentarily and involuntarily, Your Lordship."

The baron thinks for a moment.

"Well, at the very least, as they pronounce my name, they should try to see it in their mind's eye, spelled with a nice big capital 'L.'"

"That we can do," said Anselmo. "On all the walls in the attic we'll post big signs with your name written in block print, so they can see it as they pronounce it."

"Good idea. We should also speak to Signora Zanzi about the way she draws out the second syllable of Lamberto, and then clips off the third and final syllable. She sounds like a sheep bleating—*be-e-e-eh*, *be-e-e-eh*—and we can't have that."

"I'll attend to it, My Lord. If I may venture to do so, I shall also ask Signor Bergamini to be a little less emphatic in the way he punctuates each of the three syllables. There is, if I may say so, the faintest reminiscence of a soccer cheer: Lam-ber-to! Lam-ber-to!"

"Make it so, Anselmo, make it so. And do they have any requests for me?"

"Signora Merlo asks whether she might tend to her knitting during her shift."

"Tell her that she may knit, provided she doesn't count her stitches aloud."

"Signor Giacomini asks permission to fish from the window of the northern mansard, which directly overlooks the water."

"But there are no fish in Lake Orta . . ."

"I pointed that fact out to him. I explained that Lake Orta is a dead lake. He told me that he cares about fishing, not about catching fish, and that to a real fisherman, there is absolutely no difference between a dead lake and a live lake."

"Then he may fish with my blessing."

The baron gets to his feet, supporting himself with his two walking-sticks, each with a solid-gold pommel, and takes three hobbling steps (his limp: no. 8) as far as the sofa. He drops wearily onto the soft cushions, pushes a button, and listens:

"Lamberto, Lamberto, Lamberto . . ."

"That's Signorina Delfina's voice."

"Yes, Your Lordship."

"What a lovely pronunciation. You can hear each letter so distinctly, and as you have surely noticed, Anselmo, every letter in my name is different."

"Quite so, My Lord, and, begging your pardon, so is every letter in my own name."

"And in your name. And in Delfina's. I do like a name in which none of the letters appear more than once. Though other kinds of names can be nice in their way. My poor mother, for example, was named Ottavia, a name with a double 't' and two 'a's. In her case, it made for a mellifluous effect. But I was always sorry that my sister chose to have her only son baptized Ottavio. Now, Ottavio begins and ends with the same vowel. The two 'o's create the effect of a parenthesis. To have a parenthesis for your name, think of that ... Perhaps that's why I've never really liked Ottavio. I can't imagine leaving all my wealth to him ... But unfortunately I have no other relatives ..."

"No, Your Lordship."

"They all died before me, all but Ottavio. There he sits, just waiting to attend my funeral, of course. Any news of my beloved nephew?"

"No, Your Lordship. The last time we heard from him was when he asked for a loan of 25 million dollars to pay off a gambling debt. That was a year ago."

"I remember, he lost the money at skittles, moral defective that he is and always has been. Well, well, would you be so good as to make me a pot of chamomile tea, Anselmo?"

Baron Lamberto has the world's greatest chamomile

collection. He has chamomiles from the Alps and the Apennines, from the Pyrenees and the Caucasus, the Sierras and the Andes, and even from the high valleys of the Himalayas. Every variety of chamomile is carefully catalogued and stored on special shelves, with an index card indicating the place, year, and day it was harvested.

"I would suggest," said Anselmo, "a 1945 Campagna Romana."

"Quite so, you're the expert."

One day every year, the villa opens its wrought-iron gates and hardwood portals, and tourists are invited in to see Baron Lamberto's collections: the chamomile collection, the umbrella collection, the collection of seventeenth-century Dutch paintings ... Visitors come from all over the globe, and the boatmen of Lake Orta, who transport them across the water to the island in their rowboats and motorboats, earn bagsful of gold and silver.

CHAPTER 2

IT'S SIGNORA ZANZI'S SHIFT.

"Lamberto, Lamberto, Lamberto . . ."

She's very careful not to draw out the second syllable, to keep from bleating like a sheep, as she was admonished. Like Signora Merlo, she knits to ward off the boredom, and she enjoys it. She doesn't even need to count the stitches; her hands do the counting for her.

In another room in the attic, young Armando listens to Signorina Delfina's musings.

"Something about this work," Delfina is saying, "doesn't sit right."

"I think it's easy," Armando replies. "Just think if they had asked us to repeat the word 'pterosaur.'"

"What does that mean?"

"It's a flying reptile from prehistoric times. It was one of the words in the crossword puzzle last week."

"What does the pronunciation have to do with it? This work would be a mystery even if we just had to say 'polenta' or 'crème brulée' over and over day and night."

"I don't see anything mysterious about it: the baron pays us, and we do what he tells us to do. He supplies the capital, we supply the labor. The donkey pulls the cart wherever the master tells him to pull it."

"And what is the product? I worked for ten years in a stocking mill. The boss paid us (and not much, if you want to know the truth), I worked, and in the end there was a pile of stockings. What do we produce?"

"Signorina, don't make life more complicated than it needs to be. Let's imagine that someone wants to pay you to advertise Peek-Pook soap. You don't have to make soap, you just have to say: Peek-Pook, Peek-Pook, Peek-Pook. And everyone hurries out to buy a bar of Peek-Pook soap, because when they wash their face in the morning, they think they can hear your lovely little voice and they think they can see your pretty little nose."

"Save the compliments. We're not advertising Baron Lamberto; he's not for sale. We work hidden away in an attic, as if we were doing something illegal."

"Maybe it's a military secret."

"Oh, please . . ."

"An atomic secret."

"Oh, impossible . . ."

"Signorina, I've done some calculations: every time I pronounce the word Lamberto I earn five hundred lire.

That's nothing to sneeze at. The fringe benefits are excellent. The food is first class. Just today, for instance, Signor Anselmo served us risotto with truffles and Peking duck. I worked for twelve years in a refrigerator factory, and I ate bologna sandwiches the whole time. Working here, I started to gain weight, but then I asked—on behalf of us all—if we could have a gym in one of the rooms, and the request was granted in just twenty-four hours. You've seen the exercise equipment: only millionaires enjoy this kind of luxury. You like to exercise as much as I do. So what are you complaining about?"

"I'm not complaining. I just like to know the reason for things."

"And once you find out the reason, what'll you do with it then? Make a cup of coffee?"

Now it's Signora Merlo's shift. In another room in the attic, Signor Bergamini and Signor Giacomini are enjoying their break. Signor Giacomini, as usual, is fishing. He's cast hook, line, and bait out the window and he's patiently waiting. Anyone can catch a fish—the real art of fishing is in the waiting. At least, that's his opinion.

"It's like the Olympic Creed," he explains. "The most important thing in the Olympic Games is not to win but to take part."

Behind him, Signor Bergamini is waiting, too. A

coincidence that smacks of the miraculous has brought together a true fisherman and an authentic observer of fishermen, someone who never grows impatient if the fisherman doesn't catch anything, but one who just stands there, hands in his pockets, puffing calmly on his pipe, watching, and letting time go by without saying a word.

When they do talk, the fisherman and the observer of the fishermen recollect past fishing experiences, or share their opinions on any number of subjects.

"Have you noticed," asks Signor Giacomini, "that Signor Anselmo never goes anywhere without his umbrella?"

"I think he even takes it with him when he takes a shower," replies Signor Bergamini.

And in fact Signor Anselmo always carries a black-silk umbrella, dangling from his arm on its wooden handle.

"Lovely person, though."

"Absolutely."

When it's Signor Giacomini's shift, he leaves the fishing rod propped against the windowsill and asks Signor Bergamini to keep an eye on the float. Signor Bergamini is a genuine observer of fishermen: he keeps watching even after the fisherman leaves.

As he watches, he listens to the conversation of Signora Zanzi and Signora Merlo, who are busily knitting in the living room. Signora Merlo is worried. She has a cousin named Umberto and another cousin named Alberto. When it's her shift, her two cousins' names are continually at the tip of her tongue, and she's been on the verge of saying "Um-" or "Al-" instead of "Lam-" hundreds of times. Once she gets past the first syllable, it's smooth sailing, because all three names have the same second and third syllables: Umberto, Alberto, Lamberto. But for her the first syllable is always the result of a mental struggle, a fight between brain and tongue that takes place at the speed of light. Each time, she has to choose the correct syllable of the three: "Lam," "Al," or "Um."

"Luckily, so far," she says, "I've never gotten it wrong."

"You'll get used to it, wait and see. But believe you me, I have my own challenges. I think of all kinds of words that start with "lam," like lamppost, lambchop, lambaste, lamprey, lampoon. The first syllable is a snap. The trouble starts with the second syllable. But you know, it's between me and my conscience. They pay me to say Lamberto. If I said lambskin I'd feel like I was stealing."

Occasionally, down in the kitchen, the butler,

Anselmo, pushes the appropriate button and listens to the conversations going on in the attic. They keep him company while he prepares the timbale or the veal in cream sauce. He's not eavesdropping; it's just a way of learning new things. Anselmo is a scholar of the human condition.

His lordship the baron, on the other hand, would never presume to listen in on a private conversation. His poor mother, when he was small, taught him never to listen at keyholes. He only listens to make sure that the work is being done properly:

"Lamberto, Lamberto, Lamberto . . ."

Those voices give him a feeling of safety, of security. It's as if there was a guard standing watch over him, warding off enemies. He knows perfectly well that the people in the attic are repeating his name because they are paid to do so. But they do such a good job, and occasionally pronounce his name with such grace and kindness, that the baron can hardly help but think: "Listen: they really love me."

CHAPTER 3

ONE MORNING, AS THE BARON LOOKS AT himself in the mirror, he discovers that, in the still of the night, a hair has sprung up on his head. A single blond hair. There it is, quivering in the middle of his bald pate, which is checkered with brown liver spots.

"Anselmo! Come see. Hurry!"

Anselmo trots along in such haste that he forgets his umbrella, and halfway there he is obliged to turn around and go back for it.

"Look: a hair. It's been forty-five years since anything of the sort has been seen on my scalp."

"Just a moment, Your Lordship."

Anselmo hurries off in search of the big magnifying glass the baron uses to examine the stamps in his collection. Under the lens, the hair looks like a golden sapling in the bright sunlight. But there's something more . . .

"With Your Lordship's indulgence," says Anselmo, "this is not just any hair, it's a naturally wavy hair, possibly even curly."

"When I was small," the baron whispers, choked with emotion, "my poor mother used to call me her little 'curlytop.'"

As long as he has the magnifying glass in his hand, Anselmo takes advantage of the opportunity to explore carefully the entire surface of his master's scalp, in silence. Underneath the skin, he can admire the ingenious architecture of the osseous dome, nature's original model for the Pantheon, for St. Peter's cathedral, and for the motorcycle helmet.

"Here," he finally says, "where the right parietal bone meets the ethmoid, either the lens deceives me, or I'm having visions, or a second hair is coming up. Yes, I see it, it's penetrated the scalp, the tip is cautiously extending beyond the skin, it's pushing out little by little, now it's . . ."

"You'd make a first-rate radio announcer," the baron comments.

"No, I'm sure of it now: it's another blond hair. Pure silk. But no, wait, wait . . ."

"What now? Has the hair taken fright? Has it retreated to the safety of its lair?"

"Your wrinkles, Lord Lamberto . . ."

The old gentleman's face was congealed in a dense network of wrinkles, some of them fine and light, barely sketched across the surface of the epidermis, while others are creases as deep as moats. His face looked like the snout of a centenarian tortoise.

"It is my impression," Anselmo went on, "that the wrinkles are smoothing out. I remember counting three hundred wrinkles at the corner of this eye but now I'd bet my umbrella that there are fewer, far far fewer. The skin is smoothing out before my eyes. From the deepest layers young cells are rising to the surface, bursting with life and optimism, to take the place of the old cells that are sinking in a melancholy farewell."

"Anselmo," said the baron, "I see the same face I had yesterday. Two hairs don't make a spring."

The next morning, however, he is forced to admit

that his wrinkles are disappearing. The texture of his skin no longer gives the unpleasant impression of touching sandpaper. His hair, at various points on his scalp, even tufts up rakishly. His eyes, which until a couple of weeks before were hidden behind the heavy curtains of his eyelids, look out on the world with a renewed liveliness. You can see the light blue iris surrounding the black dot of the pupil like Lake Orta surrounding the island of San Giulio.

"I would say," says the baron, as he analyzes his own sensations, "that the rods and cones in my retinas seem to have awakened from a long, long sleep. The optic nerve was like a clogged pipe: now the messages shoot out and dart back to the brain at supersonic speed. It strikes me that it's early to declare victory, but one thing is certain: for many years, no doctor and no medicine has managed to give me such a feeling of well being. Anselmo, I'm starting to feel better."

"Let's go over the checklist," says the butler, pulling his notebook out of his pocket.

"All right."

"Number one: arteriosclerosis."

"We sent a blood sample to Milan for tests last week."

"Your Lordship is right. The results arrived with this morning's mail: in excellent condition. Your Lordship now has the arteries of a forty-year-old. Number three: deformative arthrosis."

"Anselmo, just take a look at my hands for yourself. The fifty and more bones in either hand have never been so agile. And that's not even to mention the eight delicate carpal bones in each wrist. They're champing at the bit to be given a little exercise."

Baron Lamberto leaps to his feet and sits down on the piano bench. He runs up and down the chords once or twice, and suddenly the robust harmonies of Beethoven's *Diabelli Variations* echo through the villa. Baron Lamberto hasn't tickled the ivories in forty-two years.

He stops playing, raises the lid, and pushes a button.

"Lamberto, Lamberto, Lamberto..."

The baron winks one eye at his butler. In the attic, work proceeds as usual.

Baron Lamberto stands up again, walks two or three steps, and bursts into laughter:

"Look," he said, "I forgot to walk with my two faithful gold-pommeled walking sticks, and I haven't fallen down. My bones and muscles are back on the job. I almost feel like taking a nice swim in the lake."

"Let's not exaggerate, Your Lordship. Let's cross out number eight, your limp, and resume our checklist.

"Number four: asthma."

"My last attack was many months ago. We had just come back from Egypt."

"Number five: chronic bronchitis."

"The last time I coughed was during Carnival, when a morsel of food went down the wrong pipe."

"Number seven: gallbladder."

"The inflammation must have taken a holiday, my dear Anselmo, because I no longer feel any discomfort down there."

They go over the checklist for several days. Baron Lamberto and his trusted manservant cover the following areas systematically, leaving no stone unturned:

—the skeletal system;

—the muscular system (that system alone took two full mornings because there are more than six hundred muscles, and they each have to be checked, one at a time);

—the nervous system (it's all so complicated that it gets on your nerves);

—the digestive tract (by now, the baron could probably digest snails with their shells);

—the circulatory system;

—the lymphatic system;

—the endocrine glands;

—the reproductive system.

Everything is in tiptop shape, from the Merkel's corpuscles, which warn the brain when bathwater is scalding hot or icy cold, to the thirty-three vertebrae of the spinal column, both the true, or movable, ones and the five fused vertebrae.

Every part of the body, every component of each part, and every element of each component is examined with strict attention, lest some malady lie concealed, the beginning of a dysfunction, the suspicion of a sabotage. The two investigators explore and reexplore the labyrinth of the veins and arteries, emerging from ventricles and auricles, mingling with erythrocytes and leucocytes.

"Your Lordship, the reticulocytes are multiplying magnificently."

"What exactly are reticulocytes?"

"Younger red blood cells."

"Well, then, let's hear it for youth."

The baron and his butler venture into the tunnel of Corti and make their way into the ear; they disembark on the islets of Langerhans, clamber up the slopes of the Adam's apple, wander through the labyrinth of the Malpighian corpuscles which are bundled together in the kidneys, swing back and forth with the oxygen and carbon dioxide that enter and are expelled from the lungs, climb over the Varolian bridge, speak into the Eustachian tube, operate the Golgi apparatus, stretch the tendons, reflect on the reflexes, feed the phagocytes, tickle the intestinal villi, and twirl the double helix of DNA. Every so often they lose sight of one another.

"Your Lordship, where are you hiding?"

"I'm just entering the pylorus. Where are you?"

"Not far from you. I'm floating through the gastric juices. We'll meet up in a minute at the duodenum."

Anselmo keeps a record of everything in the logbook. But in a sense, perhaps, all those examinations

aren't necessary. A mirror is the only test required. Any-one who took a look at Baron Lamberto would have guessed he was, at most, forty years old, and hale and healthy for his age.

A few weeks ago, he was an old man, held up only by his medicines and by his gold-pommeled walking sticks, and now look at him: a man in the prime of his life, almost a youngster, straight, tall, blond, and ath-letic. He's developed the habit of swimming around the island every morning just to stay in shape. He performs even the most demanding pieces on the piano without breaking a sweat. He does calisthenics. He chops wood for the fireplace. He rows, he goes sailing and keeps the mainsail distinct from the jib, he dives off of diving boards and, if there are none, out of trees. In the meantime, his twenty-four banks continue to send in their weekly profit reports. And all this time, in the attic of his villa, six ignorant employees, day and night, continue to repeat his name without knowing the reason why (though Signorina Delfina continues to wonder).

"Lamberto, Lamberto, Lamberto . . ."

"The old Egyptian knew what he was talking about," Lamberto muses, deeply satisfied. "Exactly what were his words? 'The name is spoken' . . . 'The name lives' . . . something like that."

"I made a note of his exact words," says Anselmo, leafing through his notebook. "Here we are: 'The man whose name is spoken remains alive.'"

"Very good," said the baron, nodding his head approvingly. "Very good indeed. 'The man whose name is spoken . . .' And it was true, considering the results of the cure. Ah, ancient wisdom!"

"If I remember correctly," Anselmo points out, "it was a secret of the pharaohs."

The baron thinks in silence.

"But the pharaohs all died. Why is that, if they all knew that saying?"

"Well, they must not have believed it. They must have thought it was just a saying of their grandparents, not a prescription that could cure all diseases."

"That must be it," the baron concludes. "What a strange character that old fakir was. I took him for a beggar."

"That's certainly what he looked like. The hovel he lived in looked like a chicken coop. There were hens perched on his head."

"Maybe they were pecking at the lice," the baron laughs. He puts one hand on the grand piano and leaps over it from a standing start. "If I'm born again, I'll be an acrobat in a equestrian circus."

"But what are you saying, Lord Lamberto? You can't die now."

"Ah, true enough. I'd forgotten."

The baron pushes a button.

"Lamberto, Lamberto, Lamberto . . ."

Every morning he has a new tooth. His old false teeth are in the garbage pail. He can crush walnuts with his new molars.

"Lamberto, Lamberto, Lamberto . . ."

"The man whose name is spoken remains alive."

CHAPTER 4

IN ROME STANDS THE DOME OF ST. PETER'S
cathedral. From high atop the dome, if you know just
where to look, you can make out a penthouse surrounded by a sprawling terrace, where a young man in his
mid-thirties sits lost in thought in the shade of a patio
umbrella. This is Ottavio, Baron Lamberto's nephew,
and he's mulling things over. He has just lost the last of
the inheritance left to him by his late mother, gambling
at skittles. Today, the tavern keeper will be sending up
his monthly bill for soda pop, which he consumes vora-
ciously, generously treating all his friends. How can he
hope to pay?

"I'm ruined," he admits to himself. "My one last hope
is if Uncle Lamberto finally makes up his mind to die and
leaves his estate to me in his will. Or at least a couple of
his banks ... He must be a hundred by now. The smart
thing to do would be to go pay a call, just to remind him
that I'm the only child of his only sister. What should I
do? Should I go or should I stay? I'll flip a coin—my last

hundred lire piece. There: I'll leave immediately."

A five-hour drive, a five-minute boat ride, a five-minute stroll through the narrow lanes of the island of San Giulio, and Ottavio is knocking at the huge front door of the baronial villa.

A beaming young athlete swings open the door.

"Good afternoon, did you wish to see someone?"

"Baron Lamberto, please."

The young man steps away with a bow. A moment later, he reappears at the door, with the same radiant smile.

"Yes, was there someone you wished to see?"

"My good sir, are you trifling with me? I asked to see Baron Lamberto. Where is he?"

"He's right here—you're looking at him. Ottavio, my nephew, only son of my only sister, don't you recognize your ever-loving uncle anymore?"

Ottavio is stunned—he faints and drops to the pavement. When he recovers consciousness, he does his best to dissemble his shock: "My delight at seeing you brimming over with health was just too much. The heart has a mind of its own. My, but I'm pleased. What's your method? Have you started a new cure?"

"It's new, but it's also ancient," the baron says with a giggle.

"It's a secret," the butler Anselmo breaks in, with a wink of the eye to his master, almost as if respectfully reminding him to watch his step.

"A Chinese secret?" Ottavio ventures.

"You're cold," says Anselmo.

"An Indian secret?"

"Getting colder."

"Persian?"

"Colder still, Signor Ottavio."

"Well, what a delight it's been to see you," says the baron. "Now you'll have to excuse me for a moment.

Anselmo, offer him something to drink, freshly squeezed orange juice, a cup of chamomile tea, whatever he'd like."

"A soda, thanks very much."

By the time Anselmo returns with a bottle of soda, the baron is back as well, in a wetsuit, diving mask, scuba tanks, and flippers.

"Would you care to come with me on a little excursion around the lakebed?"

"Thanks, Uncle Lamberto, but the mouthpiece hurts my teeth."

"Well, then why don't you make yourself comfortable? Anselmo will show you to your room. We'll see you at dinner."

Baron Lamberto moves off, leaping along like a grasshopper. His blond ringlets bounce festively in the evening breeze.

"He's wonderfully fit," says Ottavio. "You'd never guess he was ninety-three."

"He'll turn ninety-four tomorrow afternoon at 3:25," Anselmo points out.

"The situation is tragic," Ottavio thinks gloomily, lying on the bed in his room, absentmindedly counting the beams in the ceiling. "I came here hoping to find a man on his deathbed and what do I see? An Olympic champion with his muscles, teeth, and hair in place. The inheritance is slipping away. Who'll pay the monthly installments on my custom sports car? Where will I get the money to bet on skittles? Urgent action must be taken."

The first thing he does, right after dinner, is to sneak into the kitchen, purloin the carving knife that Anselmo used to slice the pheasant with cognac, and hide it under the pillow on his bed. Then he goes to sleep, but only after setting his alarm clock to go off at midnight. The alarm clock has chimes that play *The Garibaldi Hymn* by Ponchielli: *let the tombs be unhinged, let the dead rise from the earth.* After the alarm clock has chimed the hymn, Ottavio rises from the bed without a sound, without stopping even to put on his slippers, and tiptoes barefoot to listen at his Uncle Lamberto's keyhole. He can hear him snoring vigorously through the door. The time is right. He slips into the room, creeps up to the bed, takes aim by the bright moonlight filtering in through the window, and lifting the carving knife—*zac zac*—he cuts his ever-loving uncle's throat. Then he goes back to bed, without bothering to wind the alarm clock.

When he opens his eyes the next morning, he hears someone singing:

I feel so well, I feel like a king,
A sail in the morning is just the right thing

Heavens! It's Uncle Lamberto, even healthier than the day before, in a sailor's suit. There's not so much as a scratch on his throat.

"Up and at 'em, Ottavio! Let's go sailing."

Ottavio begs off with the excuse that lakewater makes him seasick, and stays in his room and ponders: "The carving knives they make these days couldn't cut a bouillon cube. I'll try again, with something a little more lethal."

The following night he tries again, with an automatic carbine he pilfered from the gun room. He winds up his alarm clock and sets it so he can get a couple hours' sleep, to make sure he's rested and ready when the time comes. When the alarm goes off, without even waiting to hear the entire *Garibaldi Hymn*, he slips soundlessly into his Uncle Lamberto's bedroom. His uncle is snoring blissfully, without a hint of suspicion. Ottavio levels the muzzle of the rifle to his uncle's heart, places his finger on the trigger, and squeezes off seven shots. As he hurries back to bed, he rubs his hands in anticipation: "We'll see this time!"

And who wakes him up the following morning?

None other than Uncle Lamberto, wriggling like a perch, and singing:

I feel so well, I feel like a king,
A swim in the morning is just the right thing

He's wearing a swimsuit this time, and there's not so much as a mosquito bite on his chest.

"Come on, Ottavio, shall we start the day with a little freestyle? Two laps around the island, and I'll give you a half-lap headstart."

Ottavio begs off with the excuse that lakewater gives him a rash and stays in to think. So he thinks and wanders around the villa. He rummages through the drawers and the armoires and looks under the carpets, in search of Uncle Lamberto's secret medicine. He even wanders into the music room, where he hears a dulcet voice emerge from the tail of the concert grand piano:

"Lamberto, Lamberto, Lamberto..."

Ottavio doesn't believe in ghosts or talking pianos, so he inspects the instrument and finally discovers a hidden device emitting a tiny voice that tirelessly repeats:

"Lamberto, Lamberto, Lamberto..."

What has happened is this: the baron, before leaving

the villa, pushed the button to make sure that work was proceeding vigorously in the loft as per terms of contract, but forgot to turn it off again. The speaker went on performing its task.

"Lamberto, Lamberto, Lamberto . . ."

"Very interesting," says the young investigator under his breath, "if slightly monotonous. Let's see where this wire leads us."

He walks and he walks, and both the wire and the nephew wind up in the attic. There he sees a pretty young woman with red hair and green eyes (with one eye on a comic book) who is reciting, in a clear, distinct voice:

"Lamberto, Lamberto, Lamberto . . ."

"Young lady, my name is Ottavio, not Lamberto," says Ottavio.

"Funny guy," replies young Armando, as he walks in. "Step aside and let me work. Delfina, it's my shift now."

Delfina stands up and stretches her arms. Armando takes her place and begins:

"Lamberto, Lamberto, Lamberto . . ."

"Signorina," says Ottavio, following the young woman into the next room, "why are you called Delfina?"

"My father was a great and powerful king, the king of France. He was a very noble old gentleman, and he wore a wig woven with gold thread. In France, the first-born son of the king is called the Dauphin."

"And why is that?"

"Because the king of France is also the king of all the dolphins. When the midwife realized that that the newborn was a girl, not a boy, everyone said: 'Oh how angry the king will be, how angry the king of France will be.' In fact, however, my father was delighted and chose to name me Delfina. An excellent decision. And in fact, by virtue of my name, I have always been a first-rate swimmer and diver."

"I don't believe a word you've said, however charming your delivery."

"And you were right not to believe me. In fact, I'm not the daughter of the king of France, but of a poor fisherman. One night he sailed out to fish on the Indian Ocean. When he reached open water, he noticed that a dolphin was following in his wake with determination. My father had a crust of bread in his pocket, which he had meant to live on for a great many days and an equal number of nights. He tore the bread in half and offered one of the pieces to the dolphin. It just so happened that the dolphin was no dolphin but the king of England, transformed into a dolphin by a wicked witch and condemned to wander the seven seas until a fisherman should offer to share his last crust of bread with him. The dolphin ate the bread, turned back into the king of England, climbed into my father's boat, asked him to ferry him to shore, and from there to the station, where he caught a train to go kill the witch."

"And how did he reward your father?"

"With a beautiful memory. When I came into the world, I was named Delfina in honor of that king of England."

"That's another very nice fairytale. But now I'd like you to tell me the truth. Why do you sit there repeating the name of my uncle Lamberto?"

"We don't know why."

"Don't tell me you've both lost your minds!"

"All six of us, if we have lost our minds, because there are six of us. It's our job. They pay us to do it. Plus board, lodging, and all the hard candy we can eat."

"Strange job."

"There are stranger jobs than this. I once met a man who worked for thirty years counting other people's money."

"He must have been a bank teller. How long have you been doing this work?"

"Eight or nine months."

"I understand."

"Then you're very clever, because I don't understand a thing. I took the job because the pay was better than other jobs. But to tell the truth, I'm getting tired of it. I have a feeling it's damaging my health. The other five are also starting to experience minor aches and pains, cramps and sore muscles here and there, nausea in the morning, the occasional dizziness."

"That must be because you're shut up inside all day and night."

"Perhaps. Well, see you later."

"What do you mean? Where are you going?"

"I'm going to bed. I got up early to start my shift, you know."

Ottavio wishes he could detain her and find out more. As he walks back out through the first room, he notices that young Armando is drawing in a graph-paper notebook. He's not drawing, he's painting. He's not painting, he's just coloring every other square black. As he does this, he repeats in a professional voice:

"Lamberto, Lamberto, Lamberto . . ."

"Here," Ottavio muses, "as our forefathers would say, something fishy is going on. And here, unless I miss my guess, is where I'll find Uncle Lamberto's secret."

As he walks downstairs, he bumps into Anselmo the butler.

"Where have you been, Master Ottavio?"

"Up on the roof, to admire the view."

The butler says nothing, but decides that he would be well advised to keep an eye on young Master Ottavio from now on.

"Is there a boat I could borrow? I need to run a little errand in the town of Orta."

"In the marina you'll find three rowboats, three sailboats, and three powerboats."

"I'll take a powerboat," Ottavio declares. "If you fail to give an engine plenty of exercise, it's liable to rust."

"Words of wisdom," says Anselmo, approvingly.

Ottavio speeds across the arm of the lake that separates the island of San Giulio from the town of Orta. He sets out to find a doctor, arranges for a visit, and tells him he has trouble sleeping.

"Have you tried counting sheep?"

"I count one million every night, but I still can't get to sleep."

"Have you tried reciting Giosué Carducci's *Piemonte*?"

"With disastrous results: the effort involved in remembering one verse after the other only keeps me awake."

"Try memorizing *I Promessi Sposi*."

"Wouldn't it be more straightforward to just take a good sleeping pill?"

"Excellent idea," the doctor exclaims. "That hadn't occurred to me. Let me write you a prescription. What's your name?"

"Giovanni Pascoli."

"How odd! There was a poet with that name."

"That was my grandfather. Poor Grandpa Giovannino."

Ottavio, in any case, has given the doctor a false name. He plans to slip sleeping pills into the dinners of all six people in the attic.

The early bird, as we know, catches the worm, but if it's asleep it can neither peck for worms nor repeat "Lamberto, Lamberto, Lamberto" into a microphone.

Here is Ottavio's reasoning: "Let's see what happens if we silence them. If what I think I've figured out is true, at the very least, Uncle Lamberto will come down with pneumonia. After that, one thing leads to another . . ." He goes on with his thinking, young thinker that he is: "If Delfina wasn't one of them, I could just poison all six at once and blame it on rotten food. But I like that girl, she's too pretty to die young. Why, I'd even be happy to marry her. But this is no time for matrimonial musings: the first thing to do is to secure the inheritance."

And so, in his mind, one plan spills over into the other. With a pocketful of sleeping pills, he heads for the lakeshore, boards the powerboat, and pulls slowly away from the dock. So slowly that he is overtaken by a boatful of Dutch tourists on an educational excursion. They're going to the island to visit the famous basilica of the saint. Conveying them across the water is Duilio the ferryman, whom everyone calls Charon to show that they've read the classics.

The tourists shout something to him in Dutch, laughing merrily. Ottavio takes no offense. Especially because a few minutes later, the boat, having bumped briefly against the wharfside on the island, pulls away as if the dock were uncomfortably hot and comes back toward him. Charon is rowing harder than ever and as they pass, he too shouts out something.

"What did you say?"

"You can't dock on the island. There are bandits."

"What bandits?"

"You go right ahead if you're interested in learning more about them, but don't say I didn't warn you."

Before reaching the dock, Ottavio passes a small fleet of watercraft abandoning the island. On the first boat are six nuns, six unfortunate holy sisters. On the second, third, and fourth boats are several captains of industry with their families. On the fifth boat is a solitary old man with his dog. They all live on the island: the holy sisters all year round, the rest of them only when the weather is nice.

"What's happening?"

"Turn back! The bandits will never let you land! As you can see, they kicked us off the island."

Among the fugitives, Ottavio sees neither his Uncle Lamberto, Anselmo, nor the people in the attic . . .

"I'm going to take a look," Ottavio decides. And he turns the prow of his powerboat toward the marina. Waiting to greet him is a citizen wearing a mask who displays a submachine gun and says:

"Welcome to the island, sir, we've been expecting you. Please moor your boat. As of today, all regattas are canceled."

"What's happened," Ottavio asks, "has war been declared?"

"The island has been occupied, sir. You however are permitted to dock, because you are a member of the family. You will be given further instructions in due time."

Ottavio complies. Can you really argue with a submachine gun?

CHAPTER 5

THE ENTIRE ISLAND OF SAN GIULIO LOOKS as if it were carefully crafted by hand, like a construction toy. Meter by meter, century after century, taking over one from another, men and other men have shaped the island with their work, their efforts overlapping over the years. There are patches of green, but nature has nothing to do with it: these are the gardens of the villas. There is no rock in sight, only stone, brick, sheets of glass, pillars, and roofs. The whole island is as tightly assembled as the pieces of a jigsaw puzzle. At night, the different shades of color vanish, the silhouettes melt together, and the island comes to resemble a monument carved from a single block of black stone, standing guard over the somber water. Here and there, a shaft of light shoots out from an invisible window, like a rope stretched out to keep the island anchored to the mainland.

Along the Orta lakefront, people count the lights.

"The lights are on in Baron Lamberto's villa."

"Of course, he's the only one left."

The reports that bandits have occupied the island have lured thousands of people down to the lakeshore. There are the inhabitants of the town of Orta, emerging from the narrow age-old lanes, from the venerable aristocratic palazzi, or venturing down from the steep mountainsides. There are tourists, who leave their dinners to grow cold on the tables of the hotels. Notable by their absence are the refugees from the island, who have tucked themselves into bed to get over their fright.

At the center of attention are the Dutch tourists and the ferryman Duilio, who were the first to raise the alarm. But the Dutch tourists only speak Dutch and no one can understand a word they are saying. It falls to Charon to answer questions.

"What were they like, what were they like?"

"Who?"

"Why, the bandits, of course."

"They had masks over their faces."

"Black masks?"

"Black, dark blue, I don't know. I was keeping an eye on their weapons."

"Rifles or submachine guns?"

"Rifles, submachine guns, and revolvers, too. And I even saw two of them setting up a small-bore cannon."

"How could you tell it was a small-bore cannon?"

"Well, I'm sure I can tell the difference between a small-bore cannon and a polenta pot."

"Are you sure you can tell one from a half-liter of red wine?"

Duilio turns his back on this impudent questioner to answer a more courteous gentleman, who asks:

"Were there lots of them?"

"Lots and lots."

"How many, would you say, more or less?"

"More than twenty and less than thirty."

"Did they speak Italian?"

"Sure. Otherwise, how could I have understood them when they told me that no one could get off the boat and that I had to head back to shore? They spoke Italian."

"Did they speak it well?"

"Well, I'm no schoolteacher, to give them grades."

"Oh, that's rich. Charon: I grade the bandits. B plus, C minus."

"But not even schoolteachers give grades nowadays."

"No, what I mean is, maybe they had an accent, you know, like Milanese, Sicilian, English, German . . ."

"Banditesque . . ." a humorist breaks in.

Duilio has already described what happened twenty times. Everybody that heard his description has in turn repeated the story twenty times to people who haven't heard it yet, but there's always someone else who just got there a minute ago and wants to hear the whole story from the beginning, so that they can repeat it for the others who will show up later on.

The Dutch tourists go on speaking in Dutch, and all around them is a crowd of people, nodding their heads vigorously, even though they don't understand a word. At a certain point, one fellow turns to a big Dutchman, whom the others address as "Professor," and asks: "Do you speak English?"

The professor brightens at this question and starts speaking in English, but the fellow who asked the question in the first place takes fright and runs away. Some of the other Dutchmen try saying a few words in German, or in French, and they find citizens of Orta who have worked in Germany, or France, and speak those languages. And so communication is finally established and the tourists are in seventh heaven.

"There was one of them who gave orders in a low voice," Duilio reports, and all around him others repeat, for those who weren't paying attention or were too far away: "One of them was giving orders in a low voice."

That detail seems very important. Maybe that was the leader. Or maybe not. There is plenty to talk over.

Suddenly, a woman changes the topic of discussion by wondering out loud:

"Who knows why they decided to occupy the island of San Giulio, is what I'd like to know."

At first, the only responses are incoherent mutterings, like:

"Yeah."

"Go figure."

"Who can say?"

"Hmmm."

Then conjectures begin to surface.

"If you ask me, it's all for the publicity."

"But publicity for what?"

"I don't know: toothpaste."

"What does toothpaste have to do with any of this? It's the middle of summer."

"What are you saying? Don't they advertise ice cream during the winter?"

"Advertisement is the soul of commerce."

"You don't think they're trying to sell the island?"

"This must be one of the mayor's ideas."

"I have nothing to do with this," shouts the mayor, who overheard. "I would have nothing to do with this sort of buffoonery."

"So you think this is buffoonery? Where have you

ever seen a buffoon with a cannon?"

"Come on! Cannons . . ."

"That's what Charon said."

"Charon said small-bore cannons."

"Maybe it's an advertisement for Canon cameras."

"If you ask me," states a tall, elegant woman, and everybody listens to her willingly because she has such beautiful eyes, "it might just be a trick by Baron Lamberto to undermine tourism on the island."

"Sure, maybe he doesn't like the sound of Dr. Scholl's clogs."

"Maybe he's bothered by the smell of Dutch cheese."

Laughter.

"Excuse me, Signora. Baron Lamberto is ninety-four years old and absolutely riddled with illnesses. Hard of hearing as he is, even cannon fire wouldn't bother him. And to be perfectly frank, he's never caused any trouble."

"A pleasure to have him as a neighbor."

"And his butler too, the one with the umbrella."

"Two excellent neighbors."

"I mean, they do seem to like their mysteries. All the invisible staff they brought with them . . ."

"That's right, they have at least six people working for them, and we've never seen one of them on their day off."

"Always up in the attic, I've heard."

"Look, even now, the lights are on in the attic."

Everyone turns to look in the same direction.

"To come back to the bandits," says a Milanese who is staying at the best hotel, "some time ago I heard about a group of abstract painters in Omegna, Verbania, and Domodossola who have issued a manifesto against picture postcards, demanding that all picture postcards be destroyed and threatening to take action."

"What would they do? Attack the tobacconists'?"

"Build postcard bonfires in the main square?"

"The gentleman means they might have occupied the island as a bargaining chip with the Italian nation: either the government destroys every picture postcard on the Italian peninsula, islands included, or else . . ."

"Well, what could they threaten to do?"

"They'll blow up San Giulio."

"Ba-boom!"

"That strikes me as a clear case of defamation. I've known many abstract painters personally: they were all responsible husbands and fathers. One was even a grandfather."

"I knew one who was a wife and mother. She was an aunt, too, because her sister was married with two children."

"I'm not going to argue the point," muttered the Milanese visitor, "I'm just saying what I've heard."

"Where did you hear it?"

"On the train."

"Oh, that's great. People ride the train just so they can tell tall tales, since no one can check their facts. Once I shared a passenger compartment with a guy who claimed he'd been abducted by Martians."

"Oh, now that you mention it, let's not forget about UFOs."

"What do you mean?"

"Flying saucers. Space aliens. They're landing everywhere these days, couldn't they have landed on the island of San Giulio?"

"If that's what happened, then Charon would have seen little green men with horns."

"Then it's dangerous for us to be standing here."

"I like the way you think. Let's go get a beer."

But something keeps them from walking away. A thrill of excitement surges through the crowd. A tiny dot of light is moving away from the island and advancing toward the Orta shore.

"Someone's coming toward us."

"A Martian?"

The onlookers who have telescopes squint into the

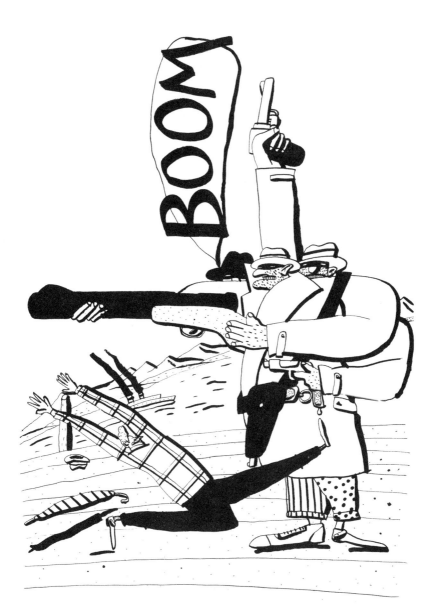

darkness, eager to be the first to provide a report about the "someone" who is crossing the invisible boundary between mystery and dry land.

"He's digging his oars too deep. He's working twice as hard as he needs to."

"There's an umbrella hooked over his arm."

"Oh, then that's Signor Anselmo."

"What did I tell you? It's all just one of the baron's tricks. Now he's sending his butler to dictate his demands."

One uncouth young man leans out toward the rower and beats time with his voice.

"Oop-la! Oop-la!"

"What are you doing?" observes an expert on Olympic regattas. "Don't you see it's a single sculler? There's no coxswain on a single scull."

Signor Anselmo—because that's exactly who it is, recognizable not only by his umbrella but also by his white hair—steps out of the boat and onto the embarcadero, panting.

"Where . . . where . . . is the mayor?"

"What did I tell you? This is one of the mayor's ideas."

"Hello, here I am. Who asked for the mayor?"

Signor Anselmo clears his throat and adjusts the umbrella handle on his forearm. This is a solemn moment. Everybody hushes one another, producing a tremendous din.

"Mister Mayor," Anselmo begins, "I am authorized to deliver the following message to you:

"'First point: the island of San Giulio is under military occupation by the 24-L Gang.'"

"What did he say: 24-M?"

"No, 24-N."

"L. Like Lamberto," Anselmo explains. "May I continue now?"

"I would be grateful if you did," says the mayor of Orta. "And all of you (addressing the crowd), stop interrupting him. Great Caesar's Ghost!"

"'Second point: the mayor of Orta is hereby appointed to summon within forty-eight hours the presidents of the twenty-four banks owned by Baron Lamberto.' Here is a list of the presidents and their direct phone numbers, Mister Mayor."

"And who is supposed to pay for all these long-distance and intercontinental phone calls? Look at this . . . Zurich, Hong Kong, Singapore . . . This will clean us out!"

"'Third point,'" said Anselmo, wiping his forehead with his handkerchief, "'the ferryman Duilio is appointed to bring supplies to the island every morning at eight o'clock.' Where is Duilio?"

"Here."

"This is your expense account. In this envelope you'll find the money. Anything that's left over is yours, as a tip."

"What if I'm not willing?"

"'Fourth point,'" Duilio resumes without answering him. "'If these orders are not carried out, the town of Orta will be bombarded from the island.'"

Nobody says another word. Matters have suddenly turned serious.

"'Fifth point. It is forbidden to approach the island by boat, by swimming, underwater, or by air. Signed: The 24-L.'"

Anselmo is done. He sketches out a bow, mutters a hasty "buona sera," turns his rowboat around, and heads back to the island. You can hear the dull splash of the oars entering the water. Digging a little too deep, as someone already pointed out.

But now no one feels like making any observations. You can only hear whispers, murmurs, people coughing. The mayor is hurrying to town hall to get on the phone. He calls the prefect, the Minister of the Interior, and his wife, who is at the beach in Viareggio. Then, with a sigh, he begins dialing the numbers from the list that Anselmo gave him.

The curious onlookers who are still looking across at the island now have the impression that it is becoming darker and more compact. The lights that once punctuated its mass are dark now. It's as if the island has cut off all contact with the mainland, and is preparing for a long siege.

This is how it must have looked, before the year 1000, to the Emperor Otto when Berengarius, the king of Italy, took refuge there, and it took weeks before the emperor could force the king to surrender. Once Berengarius was defeated, his wife Willa took refuge on the island of San Giulio, with all the kingdom's treasure. Otto was forced to begin his siege over again from scratch, and it lasted a lot longer this time: some say two months, others say three months. In the end, they came to an understanding: the queen handed over the treasure to the emperor and in exchange he allowed her to go where she wanted. Final score: one all. Old stories involving people who've been dead for a thousand years. The stones of the island, however, still remember and now they assume a menacing appearance in the dark.

"Come on, let's go to bed," the crowd says.

"Come on."

CHAPTER 6

THE BANDITS ARRIVED BY WATER, IN small groups, in a variety of disguises. A few rented a boat in Pettenasco. They wore Boy Scout uniforms, and explained that they had come from Domodossola on a field trip. Before dawn, a few others stole a sailboat that belonged to the chief physician of the hospital at Omegna. Later, people at Pella would remember a pair of cheerful and likable monks who paid to be ferried over to the island by motorboat; after paying the skipper, they also gave the boat a benediction. The skipper kidded them:

"St. Julius didn't need a motorboat to get across the lake, though, did he? He just spread his cape on the surface of the water, stepped onto it, and walked across the lake, no sails, no motor."

"We're not saints," the two fake monks replied, "and as you can see, we don't wear capes, because it's not the right season."

Once on the island, the bandits foregathered in

the ancient basilica, as if they were a group of pilgrims. The chief issued his commands: this one keeps an eye on the lakeshore, that one climbs the belltower, these others take the machine guns and small-bore cannons, the last three are to come with him, to the villa of Baron Lamberto.

They knocked at the door, Anselmo came to answer, and the first thing they asked was:

"Is it raining in there?"

"No, why?"

"Excuse me, but we see you're carrying an umbrella."

"I just like it. It's something I remember my old father by; he was an umbrella-maker from Gignese."

"Good for you, you honor your father and mother. Now get inside, lock the door, hand over the key, and summon the baron."

"Who shall I announce, if I may ask?"

"Take your pick, this is a pistol, and that's a submachine gun. Get moving."

Anselmo obeyed and hurried to the baron, who was training with a punching ball and greeted him enthusiastically.

"Watch this, Anselmo. Look at this cross, observe how I lunge, admire the feints, note the movement of the legs. Tomorrow I want you to run over to Milan, I'll give you the address of a gym, and you'll go find a boxer willing to train me. I'd say a middleweight, what do you think? Or should we look for a middle-heavy weight? As for the pay, just offer him twice what he asks, we shouldn't overdo it."

"Baron, may I speak?"

"Tell me, Anselmo. What's the matter? Why is your umbrella trembling?"

"There are some gentlemen downstairs, Your Lordship. . . ."

"Send them away, I'm not expecting anyone."

"That's not possible, Baron. They're armed."

"Armed . . . what do they look like?"

"I couldn't say, Your Lordship. They have masks over their faces."

"Masks! There must be some mistake, Carnival was months ago."

"If Your Lordship would like to hide in the attic, or in the basement, I can tell those gentlemen that you're not here right now, that they should try stopping by tomorrow."

"No, Anselmo, that's not right. You're too old to be exposed to certain risks. I'll come downstairs immediately. In the meantime, offer those gentlemen some orangeade or a chamomile tea, or whatever they like."

Anselmo went back down to where the bandits were waiting.

"His Lordship the Baron will be with you immediately."

"Exactly, that's precisely what he must do."

The baron took off his track suit and put on a pair of blue jeans and a light blue t-shirt, and he welcomed his visitors with an open, welcoming smile.

"Good morning, gentlemen. How can I be of assistance to you?"

With a nod of the head, the chief signaled two of his men, who moved off to scout the villa from top to bottom.

"Your Lordship," the chief said, "you are our prisoner."

"I don't recall declaring war on anyone," the baron replied, "nor do I remember losing any battles."

"Your answer," said the chief, "clearly shows that you are a brave man. I congratulate you. I hate dealing with people who wet their pants in fear the minute they see a gun. That however does not change the situation. Courageous though you may be, you are still our prisoner."

"Whose prisoner, if I may ask? You can't expect me to surrender to the first stranger who happens by. Introduce yourself, introduce your friends, and then we'll see."

"You," the bandit chief went on, "are a prisoner of the 24-L."

"What did you say? The 24-M?"

"No, L, Your Lordship. L as in Lamberto."

"What a coincidence! That happens to be my name."

"It's our name, too, Your Lordship. There are twenty-four of us and we're all named Lamberto."

"Pleasure to meet you," said the baron, "in fact, a pleasure multiplied by twenty-four. I never thought my name was so common. Aside from myself, I've only met three Lamberti in my life: one in Milan, one in Venice, and one in Constantinople, though he was from Forlí. He happened to be in Turkey in business; he was a wholesaler of jams and marmalades. I remember I asked him the time in the street. And do you know what he said to me? He said: "It's time to go drink a beer. Come with me." And that's how we chanced to meet. Speaking of beer, Anselmo, you still haven't offered these gentlemen anything to drink . . ."

"Thanks, maybe later," the chief broke in. "First you must listen closely to what I have to say. First of all, don't worry about the weapons, we have no intention of hurting you in any way, if you accept our conditions."

"Chief," (the two men that went to inspect the villa had returned and one of them, quite boorishly, interrupted the conversation) "everything's under control. But there are some strange people up in the attic. They claim to be the baron's employees, and their job is to take turns repeating his name, day and night. One of them is sitting at a table, saying 'Lamberto, Lamberto, Lamberto,' and he refused to stop, even when we showed him the pistol."

"That must be Signor Bergamini," the baron explained. "He's a calm gentleman, very devoted to his work."

"What's this all about?" the bandit chief demanded.

"It's just my idea of fun," the baron replied, "the whim of a millionaire. I like to know that there's always someone with my name on their lips. It's gratifying, like scratching an itch. In other words, it's just a hobby. Do you have any objections?"

"Absolutely not," the chief assured him. "It doesn't interfere with our plans."

"I'm delighted to hear it," replied the baron, winking an eye at the unfortunate Anselmo, who was white as a ghost. "For that matter, I pay them handsomely. You wouldn't want to interfere with their right to work, I trust."

"I already told you I don't," the chief said again. "In fact, it's a pleasure for us as well, because we're called Lamberto just like you."

"In fact, that's astonishing to me. Not even one of you is named Giuseppe, Reginaldo, or Stanislao? How did you manage to put together twenty-four people with this same name?"

"We put an ad in the classified section of the newspaper," said the chief. "Now, enough chitchat, let's get down to brass tacks."

"You can also say 'let's get down to business,'" the baron pointed out.

"Here's how matters stand. The island is under military occupation. The villa is isolated from the rest of the world and the Milky Way. You, Your Lordship, are our prisoner. In order to regain your liberty, you must pay us a million dollars for each of your twenty-four banks. That's a grand total of twenty-four million dollars."

"Plus tax?" the baron asked, without turning a hair. "Plus registration stamps?"

If the bandit chief answered him, no one heard what he said, because at that very moment his nephew Ottavio entered the room, accompanied by the bandit who had captured him on his return from Orta with his pockets full of sleeping pills.

"Uncle dear, what's going on?"

"Nothing, Ottavio. All sizzle and not much steak."

"Ha, ha," snickered the bandit chief. "For a line like that, I'd almost be willing to give you a discount."

"Do I strike you as the type who haggles over the price?" Baron Lamberto asked him. And without waiting for an answer, he stood up, announced that he intended to resume training with the punching ball, and left the room, followed by bandits with weapons in their hands.

"This evening you will take a boat and go to Orta . . ." said the bandit chief to Anselmo.

"I don't know how to row," whined Anselmo.

"You'll learn as you go," said the chief.

And that is how the invasion of the island of San Giulio began.

As the evening shadows lengthened, Anselmo climbed into a boat to perform the mission he'd been assigned. He was so upset that he dropped his umbrella into the lakewater. At precisely that moment, Signor Giacomini, from the attic, reeled in his fishing line and the hook caught the umbrella. Signor Anselmo refused to set out without his umbrella. One of the bandits had to go upstairs to get it for him.

"It's soaking wet," Anselmo complained. "Give me a chance to dry it off."

He ran to get his hairdryer, and he dried the umbrella inside and out. Finally he set off for Orta. The rest of what happened you've already heard.

CHAPTER 7

NOW THERE'S A SPECTACLE TWENTY-FOUR hours a day in Orta. The island is surrounded by a tight cordon of boats filled with policemen, keeping an eye on the bandits. Around this first circle there's a second circle of boats packed to the gunwales with rubberneckers and special correspondents keeping an eye on the police. All over the lake, whether the sun is shining or rain is falling, other news professionals and curious dilettantes come and go in powerboats or take advantage of the wind to do a little sailing. At night, the boats are lit up with spotlights, flashlights, carbide lamps, candles, and torches. All that's missing is fireworks, because it's not the feast day of St. Julius.

The old town is flooded with tourists who prefer adventurous vacations to sleepy holidays. There's not a single vacancy in the hotels of Lake Orta, Verbano, or Ossola. Camp grounds spring up like mushroom patches along the lakeshore, around towns midway up the slope, in the forests, and in the subalpine valleys. Journalists,

radio announcers, and television news anchors have arrived from the five parts of the world, because Baron Lamberto is famous from the North Pole to the South Pole on account of his banks. So not only the Italians, but also the Swiss, the Burgundians, the Americans, and the Afro-Asiatics want to know every last detail about every development that concerns him. There are newsmen camped out under the porticoes in the town square, and others perched on balconies and roofs. There are spyglasses and telescopes aimed at the island from every scenic outlook along the switchbacks and hairpin curves along the roads that run around the lake, both the eastern and the western shores. There are powerful telephoto lenses observing constantly from atop the bell towers of Pogno, San Maurizio d'Opaglio, Alzo, Pella, Corconio, Lortallo, and Vacciago; though not actually on the tippy-tops of the bell towers, because they are too pointy, but actually from the windowsills of the belfries.

Other points of observation that are much vied over by the press are these:

—the Belvedere of Quarna, where the beer is always chilled;

—the sanctuary of the Madonna del Sasso, perched high above the lake;

—a tavern in Valstrona, where you can't really see a thing, but which serves an excellent polenta with rabbit;

—the tower of Buccione, built in the twelfth century, but still in excellent shape;

—the monastery of Mount Mesma, where the monks are very clever about collecting rainwater, but offer their guests a savory dessert wine;

—the sanctuary of the Madonna della Bocciola;

—and of course, high behind Orta, on the highest point of the promontory, the open square of the Sacred Mount, from which, if a thunderstorm begins, one can quickly reach shelter in the chapels where colorful terracotta statues, coated with dust and riddled with age, silently recount the story of St. Francis.

The Japanese photographers, who are particularly systematic, have occupied the two highest points of the region, specifically:

—the Alpe Quaggione (3,773 feet above sea level);

—the summit of the Mottarone (4,892 feet above the same).

The Japanese, however, complain that from both those points, you can only see the lake from north to south, while there is no equally elevated and panoramic point from which to see the entire lake from south to north, unless you rule out the previously mentioned tower of Buccione, which is occupied by the forces of Mexican television.

One English journalist has pitched his tent in the woods above Ameno and from there, every morning, he enjoys the magnificent spectacle of Mount Rosa emerging from the clouds into the light of day, while all the other mountains are still enveloped in a delicate blue haze, and then summoning them all, one after the other, to take their places in the landscape, until they finally fill in all the space under the sky.

The journalist described the spectacle in an enthusiastic article that his editor in chief promptly tossed into the trash, immediately dictating a super-urgent telegram: "Forget about the landscape, our readers don't want to know about Mount Rosa, they want to know what Baron Lamberto is doing."

So the journalist wrote—for his own eyes only—a poem that begins with these lines:

O Shepherd, o Mount Rosa,
Your flock of mountains
Is bleating this morning . . .

Then he realized that the bleating was coming not from the Alps, but from a path just below his campsite, along which an old woman was leading her nanny goat to pasture. He also remembered that the poem had already been written by another poet. And that poet wasn't talking about Mount Rosa, but the Eiffel Tower in Paris. And he wasn't talking about mountains, but bridges. A dreadful welter of confusion.

That does nothing to prevent the diligent British reporter from riding his motorcycle down to Orta every morning to do his job. He usually arrives in time for the ferryman Duilio's press conference.

"What did you buy this time?"

"Twelve chickens, seven rabbits, pasta, rice, five kinds of cheeses, sixty-five pounds of fruit, coffee, sugar, and salt.

"How much salt?"

"Two packets of fine table salt and two of coarse salt."

When Duilio climbs into the boat to transport the provisions to the island, he is greeted with a burst of applause and the photographers shout at him:

"Look over here, Duilio! Smile! Hold that bunch of bananas a little higher."

The photographers address everyone by their first name.

When he gets back from the island, Duilio is followed by a procession of boats crowded with journalists, who shout questions and jot down notes:

"What did the bandits say?"

"Did you see the baron?"

"Did you see Signor Guglielmo?"

"Have you ever been in the army?"

"How old were you when you got married?"

"How many children do you have?"

"How many liters of wine do you drink a day?"

And so on, every imaginable kind of question. But the journalists, unlike the photographers, always address him respectfully.

Little boys swim behind the boat, tagging along on both the way over and the way back, delighted to be chased away by both policemen and local constables.

Street vendors show up selling balloons, peanuts, nougat, and toasted almonds. There's even one vendor selling pictures of the Colosseum, for no apparent reason. And people buy them. There's always someone who will buy anything, whatever the weather.

The bars, the cafés, and the shops stay open all night long, because people can't find a place to sleep and so they stay out wandering the streets and loitering idly till all hours, or camping out wherever they can, drinking beer and munching on sandwiches. At night, people come in from Gozzano, Borgomanero, Omegna, and Gravellone: they can't come during the day because they have to work. These commuters manage to find out everything all the same: how many chickens Duilio bought, how many liters of wine he drank. On Saturday and Sunday, visitors from Milan and Turin and industrialists from Busto Arsizio show up in vehicles and conveyances of every kind.

Sometimes when Duilio sets off for the island, his

wife is there to wave goodbye tearfully, as if he were going off to war.

"Don't go, Charon," (even she addresses him, fondly, by that nickname) "they'll hurt you, what do you have to do with it, what do you care about Baron Lamberto, think of your children, they could become orphans."

"But they're all grown up and married, with families of their own!"

"Think of your grandchildren."

"See for yourself how my grandchildren are worrying."

Three or four of his grandchildren are among the motley crew of kids diving into the lake and shouting on the wharf. The journalists ask them questions and they're interviewed on television.

"Who do you like better, Zorro or Spiderman?"

"Are you better at cybernetics or structural anthropology?"

"How much is three times eight makes twenty-four?"

In short, it's a non-stop cinematic spectacle. The shopkeepers and merchants all tip their hats to the mayor, as if it was all his idea. The local bank has opened three new teller windows.

There is always something to talk about: now a lawyer from Milan is organizing a tournament of night-time soccer matches, now a street vendor selling corkscrews is offering public demonstrations of the unequaled quality of those utensils that are so useful if you have a bottle to uncork. Then there are harpsichord concerts and percussion instrument concerts, performances by choral groups, even sack races. The local farmers remind the television reporters: "See if you can put in a good word for our wines, Gattinara, Ghemme, Sizzano, Fara ... You think mineral water can hold a candle to our Spanna?"

On the third day, an air-conditioned tour bus pulls up. By special concession of the town constable, who is impressed with the bus's passengers, the driver is given permission to park in the town square, which is theoretically a pedestrians-only area. The license plate is marked "MI," which stands for Milan. Twenty-four gentlemen step out, dressed in charcoal-grey suits. They are followed by twenty-four more gentlemen, a little younger, dressed in navy blue suits. Forty-eight white shirts and forty-eight ties all together create a wonderful impression. And who on earth might they be? These are the twenty-four managing directors of the banks owned by Baron Lamberto, each with his own personal secretary to take notes, run to the nearest phone, and carry the briefcase filled with bank documents.

The crowd holds its collective breath. Who has ever seen twenty-four managing bank directors all in one place? In the flesh, their shoes polished and gleaming, many wearing eyeglasses, and all of them wearing stern expressions.

"Make way, make way," say the personal secretaries.

With great effort a path is carved out through the mob, and along this path, in Indian file, the twenty-four gentlemen, followed by the other twenty-four gentlemen, make their way down to stand in a line along the lakeshore, within sight of the island. And then, all together, forty-eight hats are tipped, in a sign of respect. They put their hats back on their heads. They stand there, motionless, watching.

The press and the rest of the mass media all lunge at the group, shouting questions in at least twenty languages, but they only obtain answers from one of the twenty-four secretaries, who has been selected as the spokesman. And all he will say is:

"No comment."

After a few minutes, the twenty-four bankers and their personal secretaries climb up to the town hall, to the office of the mayor, who delivers to them a message from Baron Lamberto, conveyed secretly from the island by Duilio. The message reads:

My Dear Sirs,

I thank you for taking so much trouble on my behalf. I hope this finds you in good health. My own health is outstanding. Two hours a day in the gym are not enough to make me perspire. I would like to request your help in obtaining the proper equipment to allow me to lift weights, the only form of exercise available to me in my present circumstances. I wish you a very pleasant stay on the pleasant shores of Lake Orta.

Yours affectionately,

Lamberto.

Under the signature, the bandit chief has added, in block print, all capitals:

PS: IN EXCHANGE FOR OUR PRISONER BARON LAMBERTO WE DEMAND THE DELIVERY OF TWENTY-FOUR MILLION DOLLARS, ONE MIL- LION FOR EACH OF HIS BANKS. WE DO NOT ACCEPT CHECKS, TRAVELER'S CHECKS, LET- TERS OF CREDIT, OR TELEPHONE TOKENS.

The twenty-four managing directors look each other in the eye and their twenty-four secretaries do the same. They don't know whether they should be more indignant about the demand for twenty-four million dollars or sorrowful about the request for weight-lifting equipment. Faint coughs express embarrassment. Throat-clearing expresses dubious uncertainty. One of the secretaries whispers into the ear of his neighbor: "The baron must have lost his wits from the fright, poor fellow."

"Will there be a reply?" asks the mayor.

"No reply," respond the managing directors. They get to their feet as one man, bid the mayor good day, walk down to the town square, climb back onto their tour bus, followed by their twenty-four shadows and their twenty-four personal secretaries. The driver quickly conveys them to Miasino, where their secretaries have rented for them a seventeenth-century villa, with eighteenth-century frescoes, nineteenth-century paintings, and twentieth-century electrical appliances.

Here they spend the night, warm and dry in spite of the sudden furious thunderstorm that soaks the unfortunate campers perched here and there in the vast landscape, lashed by sinister flashes of lightning. One of them, however, spends a sleepless night for other reasons. He is the youngest of the twenty-four secretaries. With a rental car, he hurries to Milan to procure the weight-lifting equipment requested by the baron. The twenty-four managing directors have discussed the delicate question at length over dinner. In the end, with twenty-four votes in favor and none opposed, they have decided to obey blindly their superior's incomprehensible orders.

"He must have his reasons."

"Perhaps he's preparing a trap of some kind. We cannot stand in his way."

The next morning, as Duilio is preparing to set off for the island with his cargo of provisions and sundries, the secretary hurries back just in time to deliver the exercise equipment, purchased at a price equivalent to its weight in gold in a 24-hour gymnasium in the Lombard capital.

"What's in those packages?" ask the policemen in charge of inspecting the cargo.

"Athletic equipment, officer."

"Rather than pistols, cannons, or atomic bombs? Open up, let's have a look."

Under the curious eyes of a thousand onlookers the twine is cut, the wrapping paper unwrapped, and iron disks and metal bars come into view. A sergeant, who was an Italian national weightlifting champion, officially verifies that these are regulation weights.

"Who are they for?"

"For His Lordship the baron, officer. He intends to train in this field of athletic endeavor."

"How old is His Lordship the baron?" the warrant officer asks.

"Ninety-four, officer."

The warrant officer seems doubtful. He finally mutters something about it "never being too late" and puts his official stamp on the suspicious merchandise.

Orta and the surrounding countryside now have an excellent topic of discussion for the rest of the morning. As the news spreads by word of mouth, of course, it undergoes the occasional transformation. At noon, in Stresa, on the other side of the mountain, a waiter in a hotel tells his chef that Baron Lamberto will be competing in the upcoming Olympic games; his event will be the hammer throw. At 2:30 that afternoon in Laveno, on the Lombard shore of Lake Maggiore, an ice cream vendor tells a German customer that the baron has secretly broken the world record for pole vaulting.

"Ja, ja," says the German, licking his gelato.

CHAPTER 8

THE TWENTY-FOUR BANK DIRECTORS AND their secretaries are meeting in a plenary session in the Palazzotto della Comunità della Riviera, and it is from there that they conduct their negotiations with the bandits. It's a handsome aristocratic building from the sixteenth century that, as the guidebooks tell us, "is supported by four corner pillars, bracketing a line of stout granite columns." In other words, on the ground floor there is a portico where people can find shelter from the rain for a comfortable conversation, while upstairs there is a large hall that is reached by an outside staircase; this is an especially useful feature, because it allows the populace to watch the procession of officials going upstairs for a meeting or emerging after a meeting and, now and again, the waiters from the café bringing orders of aperitifs or, depending on the time of day, digestifs. Now there are forty-eight orders at a time: nice business. The mayor, in order to keep everyone happy, places orders with first one bar and later with another. Payable on delivery. The twenty-four bank directors take turns paying and the television reporters are able to broadcast live images of checks from, variously, the Lamberto Bank of Hong Kong, the Banque Lamberto of Monte Carlo, or the Banco Lamberto of Montevideo.

The hardest work falls to Duilio, who is constantly on call to ferry the messages back and forth across the lake. The bandits have issued an ultimatum: *"Unless we receive the ransom money in forty-eight hours, we will begin sending Baron Lamberto back to you, piece by piece: first an ear, then a finger, and so on, until we have completely picked the subject apart."*

The bankers reply that Baron Lamberto must give the order himself, in writing, otherwise they are not authorized to make any payment, be it in lire or peanuts.

The bandit chief brings this to Lamberto's attention and asks him to provide him with a handwritten document.

"Immediately," answers the baron. And he sits down and writes the following, in English, on a sheet of paper: *"My Dear Sirs, what do you say to a joyride on a ferris wheel? I herewith invite you to join me at the Prater Park in Vienna this coming Christmas."*

"Why did he write in English?" asks the bandit chief, who never studied languages.

"With my bank directors I always speak English. It's a matter of decorum."

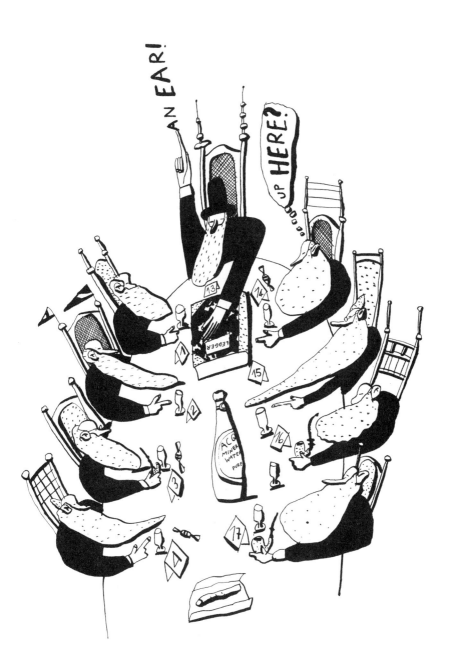

"Here I see the name of Vienna, what does that have to do with it?"

"I gave them orders to draw the money from the Lamberto Bank of Vienna, because of all my banks it happens to be the one with the most plentiful supply of Italian banknotes in small bills."

The twenty-four managing directors discuss the wording and content of the message at considerable length.

"This is unquestionably the baron's handwriting."

"True, but the style is not his."

"My colleague has a point: I don't recall the baron ever using the word 'ferris wheel.'"

"And the use of 'joyride' instead of just 'ride' hardly fits in with his personality, devoid of frivolity and ill-suited to fun."

"This text," points out another of the directors, "also contains digressions and asides that are out of keeping with the baron's lucid and focused intelligence. In fact, when one refers to the Prater Park in Vienna, one normally calls it the Große Rad, or the Great Wheel, not just a ferris wheel."

"Ferris wheel is something you might say, at the very most, about the Fair of Crusinallo."

The board votes unanimously to reject the message,

demanding one in German instead.

"Why in German?" the bandit chief asks the baron, as he shows him the board's request.

"Evidently, the director of my bank in Vienna, since he is the one who will actually have to withdraw the money, wants to be certain that he has understood correctly."

"Go ahead, write."

"And the pen?"

"It's right there."

"No, excuse me, that's the pen I used to write the last message. I've never used the same pen to write more than one document. Anselmo, bring me a new pen."

Anselmo obeys, and the baron writes, in German.

"My Dear Sirs, with this order I hereby order that all employees of my banks who do not know how to dance the tango be forthwith and summarily fired, without notice. Signed, Lamberto."

"What does the tango have to do with this?" asks the chief of the 24-L, pointing out the only word in the message that he can read.

"It's a code word for 'million.' You don't expect me to talk about money openly, do you? What if this note were to fall into the hands of some spy?"

"Very reasonable," says the chief, in an understanding tone.

The message is delivered to the proper recipients. The twenty-four directors read it aloud and the topic is opened to debate.

"The same situation: the handwriting is certainly that of Baron Lamberto. The signature is his as well. I can prove it."

As he speaks, the director shows the room a picture postcard that the baron mailed him the year before from Miami, Florida. The postcard is handed from one director to the next. Everyone inspects it and compares the signature with the one in the message.

"And yet, the style reveals a very different personality from the one we know."

"Exactly. The baron dislikes the tango."

"It may be that he dislikes it now, at age ninety-four, but liked it very much in his youth."

"I would rule that out. His Lordship, in human memory, has only ever liked profitable balance sheets, fat checkbooks, and gold ingots."

The members of the assembly burst into applause. Even the twenty-four secretaries stop taking notes for a moment and clap their hands.

The board decides unanimously that the message is unsatisfactory and that they now need some piece of unequivocal evidence that Baron Lamberto is still alive.

The bandits must now send them a documentably recent photograph of him.

"We'll give them the photograph," agrees the bandit chief.

"Anselmo," the baron commands, "go to my camera collection and select a Polaroid camera, and do as the bandit chief says."

Anselmo takes the picture, waits a few seconds, and peels apart the film. Baron Lamberto's portrait has come out perfectly. He looks like a movie star. His smile reveals all his teeth. One of his curls dangles over his right eye.

"Now," says the bandit chief, "they have everything they can ask for. If they don't give us the money, I'm sorry to tell you, the next chapter will be painful."

"Don't worry," Baron Lamberto responds. "There is a time for everything."

Duilio makes another trip from the island of San Giulio to the Palazzotto della Comunità. The twenty-four managing directors hand the photograph around without batting an eye, and wait for the ferryman to leave the hall. As soon as he does, the storm breaks.

"Treason! This isn't Baron Lamberto!"

"Aggravated fraud! False certification of credit and malfeasance: this man is an impostor!"

"Too handsome to be true."

"It's a good thing we asked for the photograph."

The thunderstorm slowly subsides. The exclamations and imprecations make way for judicious observations, well thought-out reflections.

"But if you look carefully," someone says, "it does bear a certain resemblance to Baron Lamberto."

"Where?"

"Well, for example . . . the ears."

"The real Baron Lamberto is much older. Just look."

As he speaks, the director pulls a photograph out of his wallet that depicts him with Baron Lamberto on the terrace of a hotel in Lugano. In this picture, the baron is resting his weight on a pair of canes, has the face of a tortoise, his eyes buried in folds of flesh under his sagging eyelids, and looks more dead than alive.

Everyone immediately begins rummaging through their wallets and extracting photographs of themselves with the baron, and in all of them, the baron is not an athletic young man with a vigorous forelock, but an elderly gentleman who remains on his feet only because the monsoons are not blowing.

"Observe the head. When did the baron ever wear ringlets?"

"Perhaps he put on a wig," a voice murmurs timidly.

"And the wrinkles? Where are the wrinkles?"

"With good makeup," the same voice persists, "you can do miracles. I knew a soprano opera singer who was seventy but looked twenty-five."

"The baron isn't a soprano!"

"But he likes good music."

"Well, that's true . . ."

After an hour's discussion, the board decides to demand another photograph, this one showing Baron Lamberto in profile.

"Why in profile?" the gangleader mutters, after reading the counterproposal.

"The only truly handsome feature of my face," Baron Lamberto sweetly explained, "is my nose. Perhaps you couldn't see it in that other photograph."

"That may be," the gangleader concluded, "but I'm not going to let myself be *led* by the nose. We'll take a picture of you in profile, but we'll send the picture to those gentlemen, accompanied by an ear."

"What ear?" asked Baron Lamberto.

"One of your ears. Don't worry, we have a surgeon with us. He'll do the operation to the highest medical standards. You won't feel the slightest pain."

"Thanks, you're too kind."

The bandit chief is not kidding around. Neither is the bandit-surgeon. He's sharpening a straight razor on a leather strop with an unmistakable style.

"Forgive me," asks Baron Lamberto, "but were you ever a barber, by any chance?"

"At your service, Your Lordship."

"What a relief: I can breathe now. You won't put my sideburns out of alignment."

Baron Lamberto is calm and serene. He winks an eye at the unfortunate Anselmo, who manages not to faint only because he puts his weight on his umbrella, and asks, in the simplest of tones:

"How is Delfina?"

"Very well, thank you, Your Lordship."

"And the rest of the family?"

"Excellent, Your Lordship."

Having reassured himself about the work that is going on in the attic, the baron is even more relaxed than before and allows himself a joke:

"Doctor," he says, "do you want to check for excess earwax?"

"Glad to, Your Lordship."

While the doctor removes the ear, Anselmo looks away. After a short while, hearing neither voices nor noise, he turns and sees that the doctor is bandaging the baron's head, while the bandit chief slips the severed ear into an envelope.

"We'll send it to them while it's still nice and warm," he says.

The twenty-four managing directors receive, in a single delivery, the photo of the baron in profile, the baron's right ear, and a note in which the chief of the twenty-four Lambertos has written: *"This is the first piece. Tomorrow, either the money or the second one."*

Nine managing directors faint on the spot, nine more run to wash their faces in the bathroom sink, and the remaining six are left speechless. The twenty-four secretaries take note of these proceedings without venturing any personal reactions.

The photograph in profile prompts contrasting effects. The nose is unquestionably that of Baron Lamberto. But the neck? Stout, smooth, and tan as it is, it looks nothing like the withered wattles that can be seen, just above the tie, in the commemorative photographs now in the possession of various illustrious individuals.

A doctor is summoned to examine the ear.

"Nicely cut," he says, "this is the work of a professional. You could stitch it back on in minutes and you'd never know it was gone."

"What else can you tell us?"

"Well, to my eye, this is the ear of a healthy man, well nourished, who spends plenty of time outdoors and is quite active. Age ranging from thirty-five to forty-five."

"Are you sure?"

"I'd swear on a stack of bibles."

"Would you swear on a stack of hotcakes?"

"Without a second thought."

"Then this is not the baron's ear. This ear belongs to an impostor."

"That's not my concern," says the doctor. "As far as I'm concerned, my work here is done."

"This is a fine mystery," the twenty-four managing directors say to one another. "All evidence suggests that an impostor has taken the place of His Lordship the Baron. The photograph points to it, and so does the ear. But why the devil would an impostor allow himself to be subjected to such a painful operation? Why pretend to be the baron at a time when there is nothing to be gained and so much to lose?"

After lining up a long series of question marks, they decide to sleep on it and retire to the villa in Miasino. The following morning they compare notes: one of them dreamt about white horses, someone else dreamt of the Pacific Ocean, and a few either had no dreams or forgot them. Once again the old proverb failed to deliver as promised: no one dreamt any advice worth remembering.

"Let's wait for the second piece," suggests the most prudent managing director, "and then make a decision."

The second piece is the index finger of the right hand. The chief of the 24-L, having failed to receive a positive response to his message with enclosed ear, apologizes to the baron.

"Your employees don't seem particularly concerned about your physical safety. Who's been more cruel: me, for cutting off your ear, or your twenty-four directors for ignoring the fact?"

"To my mind," says the baron, "you're evenly matched."

"Bring on the doctor," says the chief.

The bandit physician walks in beaming with his implements.

"The other ear?" he asks.

The chief explains the new program and the doctor complies with his instructions, while the baron urges: "Be careful not to cut the wrong finger. This is the index finger, between the thumb and the middle finger."

Anselmo averts his gaze to avoid the sight and catches a glimpse of the baron in the mirror, winking at him.

"How is Delfina, Anselmo?"

"In fine fettle, Your Lordship," the butler stammers.

"And the rest of the family?"

"Hard at work, Your Lordship. You know how it is, they have to make a living . . ."

Anselmo turns around: the operation is finished. The bandit chief is licking the envelope into which he has slipped the severed finger, and the bandit physician, having finished medicating the baron's hand, is about to change the dressings on his head.

"Well, I'll be," he suddenly exclaims. "Chief, look at this."

The baron pretends to be frightened. "Is it serious?"

"This is rich," says the chief, "if someone told me about it on a train I wouldn't believe them."

"What is it?" asks the baron. "What's happened?"

"What's happened is that your ear has grown back," explains the physician bandit. "If I hadn't cut off this ear myself, with my own hands . . ."

"If I hadn't put it in the envelope myself," adds the chief, baffled.

"Well," says the baron, "I don't know why you're all so astonished. Lizards grow back their tails. Prune a tree and the branches grow back stronger than ever. In autumn, leaves fall, and in spring they sprout again. The sun sets in the west every evening, and the next morning it rises again in the east. They're all old tricks that nature keeps up her sleeve."

"Perhaps," says the physician bandit, "but this is the first time I've seen an ear grow back. Have you been taking any special treatments lately?"

"Yes, I've been taking a treatment to make my hair grow back. You know, I'd gone completely bald. A dear friend of mine managed to procure an oriental remedy for me."

"Those Chinese," the chief muttered, "they invent everything you can think of. But let's not waste time in chitchat."

He writes a message to enclose with the finger: *"This is the second piece. Tomorrow morning, unless we receive the money, we'll send you an entire foot."*

At the sight of the finger, twenty out of the twenty-four managing directors faint dead away; the rest hide under the conference table. The secretaries take note of everything that happens without batting an eye.

The doctor summoned to examine the exhibit dictates his findings: "Index finger, right hand, perfectly preserved. Clean cut through the center of the proximal phalanx. This finger belongs to a person in good health, aged somewhere between thirty-five to forty-five."

"The impostor again!" someone exclaims.

"The knuckle," continues the physician, peering closely at the finger with a fifty-power magnifying glass, "presents the distinctive callus of a pugilist."

"What?"

"This means that the owner of this finger boxes. At the very least, he trains by punching a sandbag. You may examine the evidence with your own personal eyes."

"His Lordship Baron Lamberto has never boxed in his life. In fact, until ten years or so ago, he was the chairman of the Association for the Abolition of Violent Sports, and he financed press campaigns against hunting and catch wrestling. In India, he was awarded the Medal of Meekness."

"What else can you tell us about this finger?"

"The flesh presents other notable callosities, caused by the extended use of oars . . . friction from hemp ropes . . ."

"A ropemaker?"

"Sailing, gentleman. This man sails."

"A sailor?"

The directors speculate about the impostor; but there remains—once the doctor has been sent away, his fee (plus taxes) paid in full—one fundamental question. "Why on earth would an impostor allow himself to be cut to pieces in place of the baron?"

"A saint, perhaps. . . . After all, the island was named after a great saint, who chose it as the place to build his hundredth church."

"Baron Lamberto is certainly a man of great merit, a benefactor of widows and orphans, an advocate of plentiful credit, a devotee of sound finance, and so on and so forth, but that still falls well short of the idea of a heavenly intervention on his behalf."

"We should call for the parish priest."

"Where the baron is concerned, I'd call for the bishop."

"Gentlemen," a vigorous voice booms out, "let's not mix the sacred with the profane. To us, the impostor is nothing more than an impostor. Only one thing remains for us to do: reject his imposture."

"Very well, we shall return this finger to sender and accompany it with a written statement that we refuse to recognize it as belonging to Baron Lamberto."

The proposal is seconded and approved.

"Let us demand," adds another of the more aggressive directors, "that we be shown the entire baron in person."

"Excellent idea."

"That's one way to skin the cat."

"Let's hope it doesn't make them skin the baron."

"But it's not the baron at all, it's an impostor!"

"Oh, yes, I was forgetting."

Duilio is already galloping up the stairs of the Palazzotto della Comunità, photographers, and television commentators, both male and female, hard on his heels.

"What's happening?"

"At what point are the negotiations?"

Duilio holds up the sealed envelope, containing the baron's finger, the message from the bandit chief and the counter-message from the twenty-four managing directors.

It makes for a wonderful photograph, but the envelope remains a mystery to one and all. It's too small to contain twenty-four million dollars. It's too big to contain nothing but a sheet of paper.

From the heights of the surrounding hills, navy spyglasses and astronomer's telescopes focus on the envelope, Duilio with one arm raised, the Palazzotto della Comunità. The new arrivals (they still keep coming) ask naïvely: "Who is that?"

"Why, that's the famous ferryman, Duilio, also known as Charon."

"Ah, interesting. And what is he doing with that envelope in his hand? A scavenger hunt?"

CHAPTER 9

OTTAVIO, RIGHT? JUST WHAT HAS OTTAVIO been up to? He's been on pins and needles ever since the bandits arrived. They're actually prolonging his uncle's life. So long, inheritance!

In his pocket, Ottavio has the sleeping pills he'd planned to use to storm the fortress for his own purposes, by way of the attic. But he can't do a thing without a bandit tagging along.

"Where are you going?"

"To get some fresh air."

"Good idea, I'll come with you."

Ottavio walks along, cursing banditry. As practiced by others.

"Where are you going now?"

"To get a glass of water."

"You know, I'm thirsty too, let's go."

Ottavio is forced to drink the water—and he hates water—to stall for time.

Anselmo is keeping an eye on him too. If Ottavio

heads for the stairs, both of them—the bandit assigned to him and Anselmo—ask him in unison: "Where do you think you're going?"

"Up on the roof, to admire the panorama."

"There's no need," says the bandit. "Just ask me, and I'll describe Orta and the surrounding area better than a tour guide."

"I can describe it all for you in Italian, English, and German," says Anselmo. "Unfortunately, I can read French but I can't speak it. I can speak Spanish, but I can't understand it."

Also, the baron, who is forbidden to go out on the lake, is practically glued to his nephew during this period. He expects him to take part in his weight-lifting sessions. One time, he went so far as to demand that he lace on a pair of boxing gloves.

"Ottavio, let's go a couple of rounds," he says. "Working out on the punching ball gets to be dull."

"Too great an honor, uncle."

"Oh, come on, I wouldn't hit you hard, I'd just pretend."

"I'm opposed to boxing on sentimental grounds."

Try as he might, he can't get out of sparring with his Uncle Lamberto. At the first punch, he falls to the canvas and begins to count:

"One, two, three, four . . ."

"What are you doing?"

"Since there's no referee, I'm counting myself out. Nine, ten. It's a knockout, you can't touch me now."

"You're no fun to box with," says his uncle.

Luckily, one of the bandits is a former middleweight regional champion who agrees to train the baron. He beats him soundly on points over twelve rounds. The baron is in seventh heaven.

Ottavio is flat on the ground.

Then the bandits cut off the baron's ear. Then his finger. Ottavio refines his plan: he'll kill the baron and put the blame on the bandits. But no matter how much he schemes and mulls it over, he can't ever seem to find the right opportunity.

At last, an unexpected occasion presents itself. That evening, the baron presses Anselmo into service for a game of chess.

"It's time, Your Lordship," whispers the butler, as he moves his queen, "I need to take dinner upstairs to the attic."

"Send Ottavio," the baron orders distractedly.

"He's not a trained waiter," Anselmo objects, "he'll knock the salt over."

"I told you to send Ottavio."

"What are you two mumbling about?" the bandit chief breaks in, raising his eyes from the Asterix comic book he's been studying. "Silence, or I'll throw your chess set in the lake."

Anselmo is forced to ask Ottavio to take dinner up to the six workers. He does it with tears in his eyes and death in his heart. A horrifying suspicion gives him a queasy stomach. But he must obey the baron.

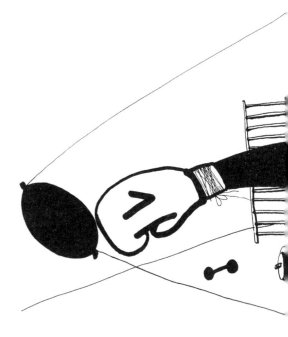

Young Ottavio is forced to implore his legs not to break into a waltz, thereby betraying his joy. If you saw him carrying the dinner tray up the stairs, you'd think he'd spent his life working as a waiter in the grand hotels on Lake Maggiore.

When he reaches the landing, he stops for a moment, pretending to give a final adjustment to the cloth napkins neatly rolled up in the drinking glasses. What he's really doing, though, is slipping a quantity of sleeping pills in the soup that would put six locomotives to sleep. There, all done.

"One thing leads to another," he sings to himself contentedly.

"We have a new waiter," Signor Armando announces to his coworkers. Signora Merlo, who is on duty, smiles with the rest:

"Lamberto, Lamberto, Lamberto . . ."

When she smiles, she gets a little distracted and says two or three times: "Alberto, Alberto . . ."

Luckily, no one notices except the nephew, Ottavio, who smiles back and kids her:

"I'm not called Lamberto or Alberto, my name is Ottavio."

The five colleagues who are off duty dig into the soup.

"That's odd," says Delfina, after tasting the first spoonful, "it tastes of cabbage, but also slightly of grenadine."

"To me," says Signora Zanzi, "it tastes like gooseberry. But it's very good."

"By the way," asks Delfina, "the other day some strange armed men showed up on the island. Who were they?"

"Hunters passing through," Ottavio explains hurriedly.

"Are there rabbits on the island?" asks Signor Giacomini, who besides being an authentic fisherman, is also an authentic hunter.

"Gray partridges, also just passing through," Ottavio replies quickly. "For the main course, as you can see, we have filet mignon with pistachios, with a side dish of creamed cauliflower, and an eggplant patty. To finish, peach pudding and Sicilian cassata."

"Cassata, they always serve us cassata," grumbles Signor Bergamini, "and never polenta."

"Would you like polenta for dinner tomorrow, Signor Bergamini?" Ottavio asks solicitously.

"Polenta for appetizer, for the main course, and for dessert!"

"Signor Bergamini can speak for himself," Signora Zanzi points out. "For the rest of us, whatever Anselmo does is done right."

Ottavio watches them eat, mentally dry-washing his hands in delight.

Midway through the meal, Signor Armando takes over from Signora Merlo, who in turn begins hungrily spooning soup.

"It's good," she says. "It tastes as if it's flavored with apricots. I'll have to remember to ask Signor Anselmo for the recipe."

And she too repeats, with great conviction: "Whatever Anselmo does is done right."

While Ottavio is there, he tries to strike up a little conversation with Signorina Delfina.

"I'd like to invite you to take a stroll," he says.

"Where, up on the roof?"

"Why, no, in Milan, in the Via Montenapoleone ... In Rome, in the Via Veneto ... In Barcelona, on the Ramblas ... In Paris, in the Rue de Rivoli ..."

"And in Carpi?"

"In Carpi ... where's Carpi?"

"Ah, there, you see? You don't know geography."

"Signorina, you always seem to think everything's funny. But I'm very serious. I'd like to give you a gift of a necklace ..."

"Of dried chestnuts!" Delfina finishes his sentence for him.

"I'd like to take you up into the Dolomites."

"Piggyback on your shoulders? Watch out, I weigh 130 pounds, even if I look like I weigh 103."

"Would you come with me to Singapore?"

What a creep! He's just finished slipping a sedative into her soup and now he's bowing and scraping shamelessly!

Now however he needs to go downstairs to allay

Anselmo's suspicions. The chess game is over and the baron has won. Now they've started a game of whist. The baron and Anselmo are playing against a couple of bandits. Once again, the baron wins. But evidently the series of victories is making him sleepy, because he yawns and glances at his watch.

"It's late," he declares. "I'm going to bed."

"I'm curious," the bandit chief says to him.

"Curious about what?"

"Curious to see if tomorrow your finger grows back the way your ear grew back."

"It's possible. Would you care to make a bet on it?"

"I'm not in the right frame of mind for betting. I have to make up my mind whether I should send your right foot to the board tomorrow or invite a couple of those gentlemen over to the island to show them that you're still alive."

"Why not just send me over to Orta instead?" the baron smiles at him. "I give you my word of honor that I'll go, show myself, and return. I could swim over, if you like."

The two men look into one another's eyes for a long time. The bandit reads in the baron's eyes a superb unruffled calm, which he attributes to many long years of familiarity with wealth and power. The baron reads in the eyes of the bandit a cold-blooded determination. This is a man who would not think twice about crushing him like a fly. His good manners are a dusting of vanilla sugar on a TNT bomb. A shiver runs through the baron. "Luckily," he thinks, "I'm perfectly safe. As long as my nerves hold out." He yawns. He yawns again.

"I'm going to bed," he says again, "sweet dreams, one and all."

"Good night, uncle," says Ottavio with a smile, as false as Judas.

"Good night, Your Lordship." That was Anselmo. The bandit says nothing.

Baron Lamberto climbs into bed and falls asleep immediately, into a tangled welter of confused dreams. He dreams that he is in a boxing ring about to begin a match. His opponent is Ottavio, but he is also the gang-leader and he smiles at him maliciously. In his left boxing glove, he is clutching a silver carving knife, in his right he is brandishing a semi-automatic carbine. Then he drops both weapons and picks up the weight-lifting bar.

"What are you doing?" Lamberto tries to say. "That's against all the rules."

Ottavio walks toward him, lifting the heavy piece of equipment higher and higher. His smile is transformed into a menacing grimace.

"Ottavio, have you lost your mind?"

The baron is unable to speak. His words become tangled in his mouth, gummed up on his tongue, obstructing his throat and nostrils, preventing him from breathing.

"Let's be done with this," says Ottavio in the dream, "I've had enough chamomile tea!"

Anselmo is nowhere to be seen. The baron has the impression that at the beginning of the match Anselmo had been acting as referee. Why, there he is now, playing bingo with the gangleader.

The baron tries to call out "Anselmo, Anselmo," but his butler's name cleaves to his palate, rolls around in his trachea, and becomes an intolerable weight pressing down on his heart.

Now Baron Lamberto wakes up in a sticky hot lake in which it is impossible to swim. Lifting one arm out of the water is like lifting a mountain. The arm comes up loaded with seaweed, dead fish, crumpled paper, and garbage. At last, the baron wakes up in his own bed. But the nightmare hasn't ended. His breathing is labored, he feels his throat tightening, sharp pains burst in his chest. He reaches out one hand to yank on the bellpull, but he can't do it. He wants to call Anselmo, but it's as if his mouth has been bricked up. Gathering his last few

ounces of strength, he slides a hand under his pillow and pushes the button that activates the speaker. The answer is a chorus of fitful snoring. No one is speaking his name. "They're sleeping," the baron realizes, "and I'm dying." But he has no time to feel fear, because he's already dead.

It is Anselmo who finds the body, already cold, at six the next morning when he brings up the coffee. Without wasting time with hysterical reactions or dramatic scenes, he pushes the buttons of the loudspeakers, one after the other. Nothing. Work seems to have stopped in the attic.

Anselmo runs upstairs, panting, and throws open one door after another, shouting, shaking the motionless bodies spread out in disorder on the beds and the floors.

"Traitors! Murderers! Is this how you respect your contract?"

They're sleeping so deeply that you'd assume they were dead if it weren't for the sound of their regular, slightly labored breathing. Anselmo delivers a series of slaps to the face of Signora Merlo, delivers a kick in the shin to Signor Armando, tosses pitchersful of water into the faces of the others, and hauls on their arms. Nothing seems to work. They wouldn't wake up if the Last Trump of the Apocalypse sounded.

"Sleeping pills," thinks Anselmo as he looks around for the umbrella that he dropped somewhere, he no longer knows where. "This is Ottavio's handiwork."

"Wake up! Wake up!" he shouts in tears. "Back to work!"

His shouting, however, has been heard by the bandits standing guard, who hurry upstairs to find out what's happening.

"The baron is dead," sobs Anselmo, "they let him die in his sleep. There's nothing left for you to do here. Clear out!"

"Let's stay calm," says the gangleader, who's been summoned by one of his bandit disciples. "Calm and sangfroid. Let's see the body."

No doubt about it. The baron is deceased. The official pronouncement is made by the physician bandit. "In my opinion," he says, "this was a myocardial infarction."

"No suspicious circumstances? No signs of an injection? Is there a chance that someone poisoned the baron?"

"I'd rule that out in the most absolute terms. The baron died of natural causes."

"Just out of curiosity," says the gangleader, "take a look at the hand."

The physician bandit removes the dressing, looks,

and clears his throat: "The finger has only half-grown back. If the baron had lived until this morning, he would have had two index fingers and ten fingers in all, just like he used to. Twenty digits in all, if you count the toes."

"You," says the gangleader to Signor Anselmo, "go to your bedroom and stay there. Two of you keep an eye on him. Where is the other one?"

Ottavio is still in bed sleeping the sleep of the just. When they tell him that his uncle has gone to his just rewards, as people used to say, he asks for a handkerchief and covers his eyes, so that no one can see that they're dry. They shut him in his room and turn the key in the lock and then head up to the attic. Here there is nothing to be done: everyone is snoring like a dormouse in hibernation and there is no way to bring them to their senses. It is sufficient to lock them in and put a sentinel on the landing.

"Now, let's think about ourselves," says the gangleader. "When he was alive, Baron Lamberto was worth the prospect at least of twenty-four million dollars. For his corpse, they won't give us a penny."

"We have his nephew," observes one of his disciples.

"He's worth even less. In his last will and testament, the baron left him nothing but a sailboat. He doesn't know that yet, but I do for certain, without the slightest doubt. This operation is a failure. Nothing remains but to take to our heels."

"And fall into the hands of the police surrounding the island."

"The pilot who was supposed to come pick us up with his plane—"

"—won't, because there's no money in it for him, either."

The gangleader views the situation without illusions.

"We have to find a way to leave unnoticed."

"Maybe we can turn ourselves into invisible men."

"Don't talk nonsense."

"We could dig a tunnel under the island, under the lake, under the mountains, and then we could surface in Swiss territory."

"Shut up and let me think."

"What, are you only one who can think?"

"You can think too, let's all think together, but no one better open his mouth to spout any more nonsense."

They think and think, but it's like scratching away at a marble wall: nothing comes loose, the fingernail can't get purchase.

From time to time one of them makes a sudden move, opens his mouth, and everyone turns in his direction, but the idea—on the verge of being expressed in words—has stolen away.

"I had it on the tip of my tongue," the man explains apologetically.

The twenty-four Lambertos, one after another, let their thoughts wander. One of them wishes he was on a beach in the Balearic Islands, another dreams of being on a hotel terrace in Macugnaga looking up at Mount Rosa. Only their chief knows how to concentrate properly. His teeth start to hurt, he's concentrating so hard. But the idea just doesn't come.

"Let's try using the dictionary," he says at a certain point.

Not everyone knows what a dictionary is, but they say nothing to keep from being taken for illiterates. In the meanwhile, their chief has taken a fat volume from the shelf, slips his finger between the pages at random, lets it fall open, and reads:

"'*Pandemonium.*' Well, if pandemonium broke loose we could make our way south to Brindisi in the confusion. Let's try another."

"The next word is: '*Lynx. European mammal belonging to the order of the Carnivora, a skillful predator, with soft fur and pointed ears topped with a tuft of hair.*'"

Then comes: "*Talcum.*"

"Magnificent," says one of the bandits. "We'll order twenty-four bags of talcum powder, hide inside them, and return them to the manufacturer saying this talcum is white and we were actually expecting pink talcum. Then along the way we can jump off the truck..."

"*Trapezoid*," the chief reads aloud, continuing to slip his finger between the brittle old pages at random, in search of a useful suggestion.

There emerge, in a shambling procession: "*Myrme-cology. The zoological study of ants*"; "*Pipe cleaner. A device made of flexible wire with which tufted fabric is twisted and used to clean the stem of a tobacco pipe*"; "*Caciotta. A soft cheese from central Italy, rounded and flat.*" Excellent for a snack, but unhelpful in terms of escape plans.

The chief persists, increasingly angry. He's no lon-ger reading the words aloud, he's firing them like so many bullets: "*Dodecahedron. Metaphorical. Simmer. Pro-legomenon. Window.*"

At the word "window," the bandits sigh in relief. At least they know what that means, without reading the definition. Then the chief reads the word "*pee*" and they all burst out laughing. They certainly didn't know that the dictionary had *that* kind of word in it. With all the jolly laughter, one or two of the bandits find that very same word in their pants.

The chief isn't laughing. He's opened the dictionary at a random page and he's sitting there, finger stabbing the page, eyes wide open. You can almost hear the buzz of his brain as his thoughts whirr around. Minutes go by on tiptoes, fingers to their lips, before he finally speaks.

"Idiot."

"Oh, there are insults in the dictionary too? It just keeps getting better."

"No, *I'm* an idiot for not thinking of it before," the chief explains.

"What did you find?"

"Come on, read it out loud."

"Don't keep us on pins and needles."

"*Balloon,*" the chief reads aloud.

The twenty-three other Lambertos look at him, baffled, with a vague suspicion that their chief's reason may have been unhinged by all the intense concentration.

"Why is the chief talking about baboons?" one Lamberto whispers to the other.

"What do monkeys have to do with any of this?"

But the chief of the Lambertos isn't thinking about simians. The word that he read in the dictionary brought to mind something that happened during the first few days of the island's occupation.

"We were in the cellars, the baron, his butler, and me. Do you have any idea of how big the cellars of this villa are? That day, I saw all of them, inch by inch, level by level. Did you know that there are five floors of underground cellars?"

"You never told us, so how on earth could we have known?"

"On the fifth floor down, the lowest one, the baron has—or I should say had—his personal museum. The only reason he showed it to me is that I was holding a gun on him. He has the baby carriage his nurse used to take him out for walks in, the tricycle he first learned to pedal on, the safe from his first bank, a photocopy of his first million, in other words, all his little personal souvenirs and memorabilia. One room of the museum is piled to the ceiling with big packages tied up with a stout cord. And you know what's in those packages? This is exactly what the baron told me that day: 'Those packages contain the most beautiful dream of my life. They hold all the different pieces of the aerostatic balloon with which I had hoped to reach the North Pole, and back then I would have been the first man to set foot on it. There are the bolts of cloth, the sections of the crew car, the helium canisters. In this file are the plans and instructions. Even a child could assemble the balloon in just a few hours.' I wasn't really listening to him, because I wasn't interested just then. It's lucky I remembered it in time. Now do you understand?"

"No," a few voices mumbled, clearly mortified.

"We'll escape by balloon."

"Good idea, so the police can shoot at us and. . . . *pfffft*, the balloon will deflate."

"We'll escape at night."

"They'll see us when the spotlights illuminate us."

"No, we'll tell the police that the spotlights bother Baron Lamberto, because the glare filters through the curtains and keeps him awake."

"And where will we go?"

"Switzerland."

"And after that?"

"And after that mommy will tuck you into bed, give you a hard candy with a hole in the middle, and kiss you goodnight in the middle of your forehead. Enough talk, let's get to work."

Not all the Lamberti are convinced, but their chief is finally sure of himself again . . . The only choice is to follow him. Anyone have a better idea? No one. Any other possibilities worth trying? None. At least now there is a clear plan of action: inflate the balloon, climb aboard, and escape to the mountains.

CHAPTER 10

IN ORTA, WHEN THE SUN RISES AGAIN, NO one knows what has happened on the island during the night, but many people do have the impression that this is going to be a special day. In the meanwhile, the tour bus bringing the bankers from Miasino arrives a quarter hour earlier than usual. There they are, climbing the outside staircase of the Palazzotto della Comunità with a spring in their step, in Indian file. There is always someone standing outside whose idea of fun is to count them: "... forty-six, forty-seven, forty-eight."

But now why are they hurrying back down the steps so quickly? Because the cleaning woman hasn't finished mopping the floor yet. They'll have to wait in the ground-floor portico. The crowd surrounds them, silent and observant. Those who have already learned to tell them apart points them out to the others—few in number, to tell the truth—who don't yet know the difference between the managing director from Amsterdam and the managing director from Alexandria, Egypt.

The most experienced observers even distinguish, with the naked eye, each individual personal secretary.

"You can come in now," the cleaning woman shouts from the balcony, "but don't throw your cigarette butts on the floor!"

They climb back up and vanish through the door. The onlookers crane their necks, looking for other phenomena worthy of study, and they see Duilio the ferryman returning from the island, having already completed his first trip of the day transporting provisions.

Charon hops out of the boat and runs toward the porticoes in the town piazza, followed by the younger reporters (the older ones are still eating breakfast on the hotel terraces).

"Where are you going?"

"Charon, a smile for the press."

"How are your grandchildren? Did your mother-in-law get over her stomachache?"

The ferryman steps into a stationery shop and, without stopping to catch his breath, orders:

"Quickly, 65 pounds of scotch tape."

"What? Sixty-five pounds of . . . ?"

"Of scotch tape, scotch tape!"

"I don't have six pounds of scotch tape, much less sixty-five pounds."

The stationer shows him five or six rolls of scotch tape in different sizes.

"I'll take them all. Where can I find the rest?"

"At the home supply store next door."

Duilio rushes to the home supply store. Then he visits the various tobacconists. He manages to buy a pound, or two at the most, of scotch tape.

"We'll help you!" shout the young reporters. And they promptly split up into teams, hop in their cars, and roar off in all directions: one group toward Gozzano and Borgomanero, another group heading for Arona and Sesto Calende, a third group for Omegna and Gravellona Toce, to stock up on scotch tape. An hour later, they are all back with mountains of rolls of tape of all colors. They deliver them to Duilio with the pride of someone participating in a historic undertaking.

"I bought blue tape, it goes with the color of the lake."

"Here you are, seven pounds of scotch tape, compliments of the *Gazzetta di Quarna*."

"Eight pounds three ounces in the name of the *Corriere della Val Strona*."

Duilio hurls it all into the boat and points his bow toward the island. This new topic of discussion keeps curiosity alive until it's time for the evening aperitif.

"What are they going to do with all that scotch tape?"

"It's obvious: they'll use it to pack up all the cash from the ransom."

"No paper?"

"You'll see, they'll send Duilio to buy paper, too."

When Duilio gets back from the island and goes running headlong for the porticoes, the crowd is already waiting for him outside the stationer's. Instead he goes into the hardware store, holds up a skinny steel chain, and orders: "Five hundred yards of chain of this gauge."

"I can give you five hundred screwdrivers," says the shop owner, 'five hundred nail hooks, or five hundred shovels. My hardware store has the most complete assortment of Lake Orta. But a steel chain, it just so happens, of that exact gauge, is something we are fresh out of. I can order it, you'd have it in a couple of days."

"I need it immediately," Duilio retorts. "Tell me where I can find it."

"Why don't you take five hundred hammers?" the shopkeeper insists. "Look, I also have five hundred pairs of tongs, five hundred pairs of pliers . . ."

He wheedles, begs, cajoles. No one has ever left his hardware store empty-handed. Duilio, however, is immovable. That's a figure of speech, of course, because he gets moving immediately and goes in search of the mayor.

"Mister Mayor, thus and such and this and that: what would you recommend?"

"I would recommend Signor Giuseppe from Omegna."

Signor Giuseppe is famous for finding anything you need in the time it takes to recite the *La Cavallina Storna*. You can ask him for a 1913 Fiat, a cannon from the Great War, a Sun King costume, a chariot from the reign of the emperor Nero, a chicken-plucking machine: without blinking an eye, he sets out and finds it. For him to find half a kilometer of steel chain would be a walk in the park.

During the course of the day, before nightfall, in order to satisfy the bandits and fill Duilio's boat with new cargo, Signor Giuseppe finds:

—twenty-four wicker laundry baskets;

—a long-handled chestnut roasting pan with holes in it;

—the complete works of the German philosopher Immanuel Kant;

—a topographic map of the Alps;

—an earthenware piggy bank that moves its piggly tail in gratitude when you insert a coin in the slot.

The bandits, of course, need a variety of materials to complete their work on the balloon that they're secretly building, but in order to throw everyone off their tracks, they also make requests for objects that have nothing to do with aeronautics. That objective has been achieved. In the Palazzotto della Comunità, where the bankers and their secretaries are in permanent session, no one has any better idea of what's happening than before. They're still waiting for a response to their demand to see Baron Lamberto in the flesh and in person, and what they get is a request for a bean sieve. They fear that they will receive, from one minute to the next, a beautifully wrapped package containing one of the baron's feet—which is exactly what the bandits have threatened—and instead they are obliged deliberate on whether to accept an order for a carton of lollipops.

The hours pass. The situation becomes increasingly odd. The sun is already setting over the mountains to the west. A chill evening breeze is sweeping across the lake. Along the Orta lakeshore, anyone who has a sweater is wearing it. In the bars, the number of orders for beer and ice cream drops as the orders for hot drinks increase. The day has been full of unexpected events and incomprehensible objects, but the negotiations haven't budged.

Then night falls well and truly, and nothing remains

to be said, you couldn't argue that it wasn't dark. It's a moonless night. In the darkness, the island of San Giulio—its coastline dimly illuminated by the spotlights of the besieging forces (the intensity of the spotlights turned down to keep from disturbing the baron's sleep)—seems like an island of ghosts, it gives a person the shivers just to look at it.

At a certain hour, a reporter standing sentinel in the main square of Orta thinks he sees a large black shadow looming over the villa's roof. But he's so young that no one pays him any mind. His older colleagues don't even poke their noses outside of the warm café where they are holed up playing poker.

"A black shadow, you say? Maybe it's the devil."

"Did you check to see if it had horns?"

"Was there a whiff of brimstone?"

After a while, not even the young reporter sees the shadow anymore.

"I thought it was right there, on top of the roof. It must have been an optical illusion."

Instead, of course, it was the balloon taking flight. No one sees it rising through the darkness, with the 24-L's huddling under its belly, in the twenty-four wicker laundry baskets. The *inverna*, the chilly wind that blows across the lake from the south, pushes the balloon

toward the mountains of the Valle d'Ossola. Its silent navigation through the night is completely untroubled. In a few hours it could cross the border without even glimpsing it, and enter Swiss air space without paying customs. It *could* . . . But matters, at a certain point, decide to take a new drift. On one of those mountains there is a Boy Scout encampment. Those meritorious young men have chosen to launch a series of signal flares at exactly midnight to communicate with another group of Boy Scouts who have pitched their tents on a neighboring peak. One of the flares brightly illuminates the solemn aerostat and its twenty-four baskets. The second one unintentionally grazes the balloon and sets it on fire.

At that moment, fortunately, the balloonists are only a few dozen yards over the mountain peak. The fire spreads slowly. As a result, before the balloon can explode, the twenty-four Lambertos are able to scramble to the ground and surrender to the Boy Scouts, whom they have taken for policemen. Once they've surrendered, too bad for them, it's too late to yell "no fair!"

The news bounces for a few hours from one ham radio operator to another without making its way into official channels. An amateur radio operator in Domodossola, who has failed to understand exactly how matters stand, does manage to transmit a report that flying saucers have landed on Mount Moro. Another opera-tor in Locarno, at the northern tip of Lake Maggiore, receives only a garbled transmission and transmits the news that twenty-four Boy Scouts were eating sausages in the Val Vigezzo. The ham radio operators of Pied-mont, Lombardy, and the Canton Ticino are all man-ning their equipment and there is a dizzying welter of communications, in a confusion of "over and out" and "do you read me?" until no one understands what is go-ing on.

It is almost dawn when the report—finally clear and unambiguous— reaches Orta: the gang of the twenty-four Lambertos had been captured without a shot fired, at an elevation of 6,500 feet above sea level, by a group of little boys in shorts. Orders are immediately issued, countermanded, and reissued. A police speedboat, packed with armed men, cautiously edges over to the island . . . whereupon the shutters of a window in the villa are flung open with a crash and the disheveled head of the butler Anselmo appears, shouting a series of in-comprehensible statements.

"What did you say? A little louder, if you please!"

Anselmo also shakes the umbrella in the air, as if that had the power of amplifying his weak voice, ren-dered hoarse by the various hardships and frights.

"The baron is dead!" he shouts. "Send a carpenter right away to make a casket!"

Poor Anselmo. It took him an entire day to remember that the room where the bandits locked him is directly above the utility closet. He toiled all night long to carve a hole in the floor so that he could lower himself into the utility closet and make his way to the window. He's covered with plaster, dusty from head to foot, and his hands are bleeding

"The baron has died!" he shouts. "What on earth are you doing? Don't get any closer or they'll open fire! These people will stop at nothing!"

"Stay calm," a policeman shouts back. "Stay calm, the emergency is over! The bandits have been captured."

Anselmo doesn't stop to hear another word. He runs up to the attic to resume his quarrel with those six sleepyheads. There is no way to resume the discussion, however, because they continue to sleep like so many innocent babies. All that Anselmo can do is write in block letters on a sheet of paper, which he then places prominently, so that they'll be able to read it the moment they awaken:

BECAUSE OF YOU, BARON LAMBERTO IS DEAD. YOU'RE ALL FIRED ON THE SPOT.

Then he runs to open the bedroom where young Ottavio is being held prisoner. He, on the other hand, is sleeping like a particularly wicked baby.

"What time is it?" he asks, yawning, when Anselmo throws open the windows.

"Five thirty."

"In the afternoon?"

"In the morning, in the morning! Hurry, get out of bed."

"What for? At this hour of the morning there can't be anything urgent to do."

"Have you forgotten that His Lordship the Baron, your uncle, is dead?"

"Right," says Ottavio. "We'll have to arrange for a maritime funeral."

CHAPTER 11

YEARS WILL PASS AND CENTURIES WILL go by before the light-blue waters of Lake Orta will see another funeral like Baron Lamberto's—it was prettier than a color movie. The weather that day seemed to be doing its best to be memorable. The light was like molten silver. The circle of mountains raised their green and azure curtains and behind their peaks loomed Mount Rosa, like a giant peering over the shoulders of mere mortals.

Near and far, standing on the lakeshore or perched on the hillsides—some higher, others lower—how many bell towers are there around Lake Orta? More than thirty, without a doubt. And all of them, beginning at dawn, were solemnly pealing their bells. And in every belfry, there was a sexton or an altar boy enjoying the spectacle

Fifty thousand people have gathered along the eastern lakeshore, and just as many line the western shoreline. The promontory on which the city of Orta perches is so crowded with people that, if it were not a piece of solid rock, it would probably sink under the weight. Baron Lamberto was already famous before the island was occupied by bandits. He was already famous when he was alive. So you can imagine, now that he's dead.

The corpse is to be transported by boat from the island to Orta, and from there it will be taken to Domodossola, where Baron Lamberto is to be buried in the family vault.

There's no more than 400 yards of lakewater between the island and Orta: not far enough for the funeral procession to stretch out in its full length. It was therefore decided that it should not proceed along a straight line, but instead wind its way in a broad series of curves, moving slowly in picturesque meanderings, like certain Chinese bridges that, in order to go from point A to point B, follow a zigzagging itinerary so that those who cross them can admire the panorama from a variety of vantage points.

Leading the procession is a barge carrying priests and altar boys. Among them, we note the grandsons of Duilio the ferryman, who always seem to pop up everywhere. They're so full of energy that you almost expect to see them go scampering across the surface of the water without sinking. They fight over the aspersory filled with holy water, the aspergillum for sprinkling it, and the censer, and they get more than a few smacks in the back of the head from the assistant parish priest.

The barge is followed by twenty-four boats, all identical, each of which carries the managing director of one of the banks and his personal secretary, for a total of forty-eight functionaries dressed in black, with somber expressions on their faces. The fact is that when they reached the island, Baron Lamberto had already been nailed into his coffin.

"But what about us?" they say.

"And what about you?" asks Ottavio, shameless.

"Well, it's only natural . . . we'd have liked to pay our respects to the deceased . . . if nothing else, identify the baron in our official capacity . . ."

"The identification has been performed by the family members, that is, me, his only nephew, and his butler, Anselmo."

So the twenty-four managing directors are left to mull over their suspicions, and as the funeral wends its way across the lake, they wonder whether the casket really contains the baron or a mysterious impostor. And if the latter, where is the real baron?

Following the bankers comes the barge carrying the coffin. At the helm is Diulio, jocularly known as Charon, and today playing the part of an authentic ferryman of dead souls. The barge flies a black banner with a large golden "L" at its center. In the wake of the barge follow two small rowboats. In one, the nephew Ottavio pretends to sob into a white handkerchief with black edging. Actually, if he weren't afraid of losing his balance, he would be dancing a jig of happiness: in just a few hours he'll finally learn how much of his uncle's vast estate will wind up in his cash-starved pockets. In the other small rowboat, standing erect, leaning on his trim and dignified black umbrella, is Anselmo, brooding over his suspicions about the nephew Ottavio. But who would believe him, if he openly accused him? All right, he might be able to prove that it was Ottavio who slipped the sedatives into the dinner of the inhabitants of the attic. So what? What physician, what criminal judge would ever believe that what killed the baron was not having his name pronounced? They'd look at him as if he were crazy. Maybe they'd say: "Are you trying to palm off the story of the fakir on us? You realize that we live in the twentieth century?"

Anselmo weeps. Even from far away, if someone has a precision-made navy spyglass in hand, they can see the big salt tears rolling down his cheeks and plopping onto the umbrella.

Other boats follow in their wake, bearing authorities

and officials of all kinds, both civilian and military, national and foreign. Then come the boats flying the banners of the associations to which Baron Lamberto was a benefactor, great public philanthropist that he's always been: the Bocce Society of Orta, the Union of Anglo-Prussian Banks, the Association of the Friends of High Finance, the Society for the Advancement of Internal Revenue, the Juventus Athletic Club of Armeno, and so on. The banners form a lovely composition of bright colors.

Then come 127 motorboats piled high with wreaths and floral arrangements from all five of the earth's continents. There's even one from Tierra del Fuego. Just counting the wreaths is a big job for the onlookers. Some count a few extra, others count a few less. To avoid a quarrel, they agree on a total number of 320 wreaths. Still, there's a diminutive, tightly wound gentleman who insists there are 321. There's always a freethinker who is reluctant to go along with the majority view.

Meanwhile, whispers and hisses, questions and answers, exclamations and comments fly from the tens of thousands of mouths lining the lake:

"Poor Baron Lamberto, even with all the money he had. . . ."

"Eh, Lamberto, he was rich all right."

"Lamberto was good-hearted, too."

"Who? Lamberto? As good as gold."

"But was this the Lamberto that . . ."

"That's right. The very same Lamberto."

"Well, which Lamberto did you think it was?"

"There's only one Lamberto. Or there used to be."

"There once was a baron named Lamberto."

Bringing up the rear of the procession is a broad barge loaded with musicians. It's the band of the trolley conductors of Milan, brought here specially by train, and they're playing one funeral march after another.

"Baron Lamberto was a true music lover."

"Lamberto loved all things beautiful and good."

"True, Lamberto had a heart . . ."

"What did you say? Lamberto died of heart disease?"

"I said that Lamberto had a big heart."

"Poor Lamberto."

"Lamberto here."

"Lamberto there."

"Lamberto up."

"Lamberto down."

"Lamberto above and below."

"Lamberto, Lamberto, Lamberto."

If a listener could float up to a point sixty-five thousand feet above the heads of the crowd and if at that point all the words that are now being uttered by all those people on the lake and around the lake converged, we may suppose that he, the listener, would be treated to an uninterrupted succession of:

"Lamberto, Lamberto, Lamberto."

It is true, of course, that the people are speaking of other things. While they are watching the funeral, the industrialists of Omegna speak of espresso makers and egg whisks; the manufacturers of sinks and faucets in San Maurizio d'Opaglio exchange information about the Arab sheiks who have ordered a shipment of solid-gold faucets; the umbrella-makers of Gignese are sighing about the weather, excessively dry, at least for their tastes, this summer; the inhabitants of the mountain villages of the Valstrona are discussing the price of lumber; the abstract painters of Verbania are maligning their figurative colleagues and vice versa. But the fact remains that there is always one, at least one, person mentioning Lamberto's name, and by the time they have reached the 'o' at the end of the name, someone else is beginning to pronounce the 'l.' Nobody planned it out that way, but the fact remains that one hundred thousand or one hundred fifty thousand people, out loud or under their breath, male or female, are taking turns pronouncing that name: "Lamberto, Lamberto, Lamberto."

Suddenly—but it was inevitable, it was to be ex-pected, it would have been worth wagering on!—a se-ries of vigorous thumps and knocks emerge from the coffin. Everyone turns in that direction. The priests and the altar boys stop singing. The band stops playing. People hold their breath. The thumping and knocking gets louder. A few people faint from excitement, others tough it out: there'll be plenty of time to faint later… Finally, with a resounding crack, the coffin lid lifts, lifts a little more, flips open entirely, and splashes into the lakewater, while Baron Lamberto gets to his feet, looks around, and shouts: "You've got it all wrong! Charon, take me back home! Anselmo, look out, you're dropping your umbrella! Ottavio, where are you running off to?"

As soon as Ottavio realizes the new state of affairs, he dives over the side of his rowboat and swims vigor-ously toward the shore.

Baron Lamberto continues to shout cheerfully:

"You've got it all wrong! Start over from scratch! The funeral is postponed to a date still to be determined, because the dead man refuses to participate!"

From Orta and the surrounding area, a vast, long drawn-out syllable rises skyward: "Oh!"

Followed by a vast, long drawn-out: "Ah!"

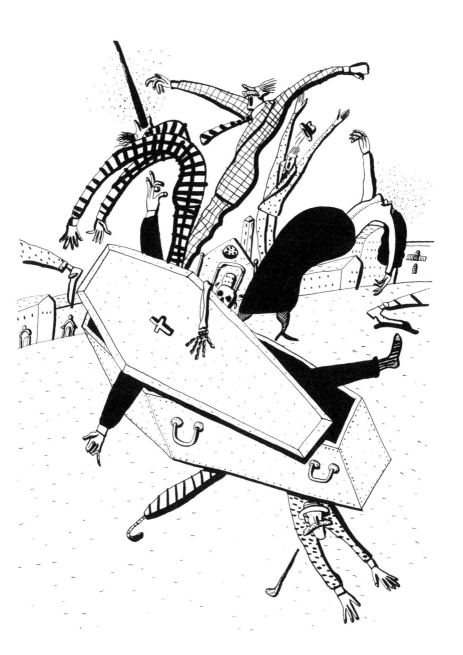

Then a thunderous burst of applause and choruses of cheers: "Long live Lamberto!"

"Thank you! And in fact, I am alive!"

The conductor of the trolleymen's band refuses to allow himself to be caught off guard by the unexpected events. He raises his baton and the hundred and twenty musicians of the celebrated woodwind and brass ensemble strike up the "Triumphal March" from *Aida*.

In his astonishment, Anselmo has dropped his umbrella. He fishes it out of the lake, opens it, refurls it, he no longer knows what he's doing.

"Lord Lamberto," he cries, "what would you like for lunch today? Would you prefer pigeons *à la* Cavour or a duck *alla mantovana*?"

The baron pays no attention to him. He's too absorbed in enjoying his celebration. And at this very moment, our theoretical listener poised sixty-five thousand feet in the air over Orta, at the point of convergence of all the voices and words rising from the shores of Lake Orta would have heard, recurring with greater force and intensity even than before: "Lamberto, Lamberto, Lamberto."

"So Lamberto is alive after all."

"Lamberto's must have been nothing more than a case of apparent death."

"Lucky Lamberto!"

"But let's admit it: Lamberto deserved it."

"Lamberto here."

"Lamberto there."

In the general air of exultation, the twenty-four managing directors and their twenty-four personal secretaries stand out by contrast. They aren't shouting, they aren't speaking, they don't give the least sign of joy. They focus their forty-eight plus forty-eight eyes upon Baron Lamberto, they scrutinize his physique, they study his physiognomy, they compare it with their memories, with the photographs in their possession, which they constantly pull out of their wallets as they look at one another, consulting each other with silent glances. Finally they order their boatmen to turn toward the island, in the wake of Charon who is already mooring his boat to the pier.

As Baron Lamberto steps out of the boat, he turns to wave to the crowd once again, clasping both hands above his head in the traditional gesture of a victorious boxer.

"Long live Lamberto!" the crowd shouts back.

Then the crowd slowly begins to melt away, because there is nothing left to see. The spectators go home contented, however, because this is the first time in the history of the lake that a funeral has had a happy ending.

There are still a few minor scuffles midway between the island and Orta, where the coffin is bobbing in the water and aficionados are quarreling over the last scraps of wood, which they mean to save as souvenirs of this fine day.

Ottavio, by now, is far away. He only stops in Florence to fill up his gas tank. It's unlikely we'll ever hear his name mentioned again, on the green shores of Lake Orta. Ciao, Ottavio.

CHAPTER 12

DELFINA IS THE FIRST TO WAKE UP AFTER two days and three nights of involuntary sleep. She doesn't immediately realize that she's woken up; in fact, she feels as if she's started a new dream, in which a band floats down from the clouds playing the "Triumphal March" from *Aida*. She isn't sure whether what's filtering down through the small high attic window are shafts of sunlight or the blare of trumpets. Her eyes are open, but that proves nothing, in a dream your eyes are always open, except when you're dreaming that your eyes are closed. She stretches her arms and legs and kicks a chair with one foot. Ouch! This bed is hard as a rock . . .

Delfina looks around and sees Signora Merlo stretched out on the floor, her head under the table. Finally, it dawns on her that she too is lying flat on her back on the floor and she leaps to her feet, as if something had just stung her.

She runs to look out the little window and sees a huge celebration underway on the lake.

TIC TAC TIC TAC TIC TAC TIC TAC TAC TIC TAC TIC TAC TIC

She runs to look at the table and finds the note that Anselmo wrote: *Baron Lamberto is dead . . . your fault . . . fired on the spot.*

"What? What? Signora Merlo! Signora Zanzi!"

With a hail of pinches, slaps, glassfuls of water poured down collars, and shouts, she manages to awaken her five coworkers."

"Is it my shift?" mutters Signor Giacomini. And still yawning, he immediately sets to work: "Lamberto, Lamberto, Lamberto."

"Stop!" cries Delfina. "Halt! There's nothing left to

lambertify. We've been fired, look at this. We may even stand accused of lamberticide. Signor Armando, please don't fall back to sleep."

"What time is it?" mutters Signor Armando.

"Maybe you should ask what day it is."

Signor Armando looks at his watch, which not only tells the time but what day of the month it is.

"By Jove! How long did we sleep? In other words, what's happened?"

"It sounds to me like a fanfare of the Carabinieri," says Signor Bergamini. "Nice trumpets."

"It's the 'Triumphal March' from *Aida*," Delfina corrects him,

"I once met a lady in Treviso named Aida. She ran a trattoria and was quite a good cook. By the way, aren't you hungry? What's for lunch today?"

"Signor Bergamini, you still don't understand the situation. And to tell the truth, neither do I. Let's see if we can find someone to explain it to us."

In full agreement, they all go downstairs and walk into the big front hall of the villa just in time to see the door flung open and a crowd pour in, shouting festively. There are policemen and town constables.

"Heavens," whispers Signora Merlo, "you don't think they're here to arrest us, do you?"

Signor Giacomini says, "I'm not saying a word without my lawyer."

Signora Zanzi proclaims, "I don't know a thing. I was sleeping."

"What, And I suppose we weren't?"

"How would I know? When I sleep, I don't look around to see what everyone else is doing."

Here comes Signor Anselmo, cheerful as a cricket. He runs up to Delfina and gives her a hug, bumping her with his umbrella.

"My dear, dear Signorina Delfina, this is the most wonderful day of my life."

"So we're not fired on the spot?"

"Forget about that! You're all rehired on the spot. In fact, I wouldn't be a bit surprised if His Lordship the Baron, in celebration of the event, didn't give you a raise."

"Just a minute. His Lordship isn't dead?"

"Lord Lamberto is more alive than ever."

"And the note?"

"As if it had never been written."

"Then let's go back upstairs," Signor Bergamini suggests. "Is lunch ready yet?"

"Not so fast," says Delfina, "I want a clear picture of what's going on here."

"Why a picture?" asks Anselmo, with great contentment. "You can see the baron himself, coming through the front door."

Baron Lamberto is entering the villa, to great applause. He's smiling, as brisk and fresh as a spring morning. All six stare at him, eyes wide open. That's the baron? What ever happened to the old gentleman with wrinkled parchment for skin, so like a tortoise, that they met a few months ago, when they were hired?

They remember him clearly, the faltering ancient, with his thin reedy voice that was always on the verge of cracking ... As he told them, supporting his weight on two canes with solid-gold pommels, turning his little eyes peeping out from beneath the cascade of eyelids: "Pay close attention, my name must be pronounced clearly ... Don't shout it ... don't whisper it ... don't sing it ... Give every syllable its proper emphasis ... Shall we give it a try, first all together and then one at a time ... Ready? Go ... Lamberto, Lamberto, Lamberto."

"How young he looks," observes Signora Zanzi.

"He really looks like another person," adds Signor Armando.

Delfina is looking increasingly grim. She does not smile even when the baron bows low to bestow a kiss on her hand, saying:

"May I say that you are lovelier every time I see you?"

"It strikes me," says Delfina seriously, "that at this point you owe us an explanation, not flattery. We have even been accused of causing your death."

"A temporary death," the baron smiles, "nothing serious."

"So much the better for you," says Delfina "but now it's time for you to tell us everything you neglected to tell us last time."

"You want to know too much," the baron sighs. "What if I doubled your pay?"

Signora Zanzi has already opened her mouth to thank the baron profusely, but Delfina is too fast for her: "We want to know the reason for the work we do. What it's for. What it produces. What it has to do with your life and your death."

The baron sighs again. Signor Anselmo, scandalized at Delfina's behavior, tries to interfere, but the baron prevents him.

"Now, now, Anselmo," he says. "Signorina Delfina has a valid point. She's not only lovely, she's very intelligent. I would like to know if the others are in agreement with her . . ."

The others look at the floor, sighing. They don't

know exactly what they should say. But they can't go against Delfina.

"All right," the baron concedes. "I'll tell you everything."

But for the moment, he can't say a thing because the twenty-four managing directors of his banks are arriving, followed by their twenty-four personal secretaries, carrying their briefcases. They march along three by three, with a military gait, determined to see the baron face to face and up close. The crowd parts to let them through. They surround the baron with a menacing air. The managing director of the Lamberto Bank of Singapore, who is the senior member of the group and is authorized to speak for the others, says: "Sir, could we speak in private?"

The baron looks at the bankers, one by one, in surprise. They seem less than pleased at his rebirth. Why ever not?

"Anselmo," he says, "accompany Signorina Delfina and her friends up to the attic. I'll join them there in a moment. To all the other ladies and gentlemen, my sincerest gratitude and my cordial wish that we may meet again. As you can see, I have a business meeting . . . Very well, we're alone now. That is, there are only forty-nine of us. Who wishes to speak?"

"I do," says the managing director from Singapore.

"Be my guest."

"I'll be brief. In fact, I'll be inquisitive. Why do you happen to have two ears?"

"I believe I have every right. Even cats have two ears."

"Then whose ear was it that the bandits delivered to us?"

"Mine."

"In that case, you had three ears, not two."

"Let me tell you . . ."

"Show us your hands, please," the managing director interrupts him.

The baron complies with the request, taking a look himself. Look at that! The amputated finger has grown back completely, in its proper place as if nothing had happened.

"Why do you happen to have ten fingers?"

"And just how many fingers do you have? And the other gentlemen, how many do they have? And how many fingers does the Pope in Rome have?"

"Leave His Holiness out of this. You are an impostor!"

"I have to admit," Baron Lamberto acknowledges with a smile, "that the facts are somewhat peculiar and unusual."

"And you are right to do so," the managing director from Singapore interrupts him again. "As for us, we refuse to recognize you as Baron Lamberto, owner and chairman of the banks that we represent."

"Then who do you think I am?"

"That's your business, my good sir. Your identity documents are of no interest to us. And you will answer to the police for the disappearance of Baron Lamberto."

"Hear, hear," cry the other twenty-four managing directors in chorus.

The twenty-four personal secretaries hasten to take note of this important retort.

Baron Lamberto smiles. Not at the retort, nor at the threat to bring the police into the matter. Something has just occurred to him. And that's what's making him smile.

"Gentlemen," he says, leaping to his feet and hurrying toward the staircase, "I'm sure you'll be kind enough to wait here for a minute or two. I just remembered something of crucial importance. While you're waiting, I'll ask my butler to provide you with refreshments."

"What on earth do you think you're doing?"

"Where are you going? Come back here!"

"Stop that impostor!"

Twenty-four plus twenty-four indignant men in

suits chase after Baron Lamberto, shouting as they go, while he gallops up the stairs, taking them three at a time, throws open the door to the attic, rushes up to the small knot of coworkers waiting there, and cries: "Signorina Delfina, would you like to marry me?"

"I beg your pardon?"

"I asked you if you'd like to marry me. Wouldn't that be simply magnificent? It occurred to me just now, as I was having a discussion with these gentlemen. Since the day I met you, my heart beats only for you, my eyes see nothing but your green eyes and your red hair. I sense that we were made for one another and that we'll live happily and contentedly forever after."

Signora Zanzi and Signora Merlo embrace joyfully, saying that they'd long expected this. Signor Armando is shocked, because to tell the truth he's been having warm thoughts of his own about Signorina Delfina. Signor Bergamini and Signor Giacomini clap their hands and venture a little light raillery:

"Is that the sound of wedding bells?"

"Long live Baroness Delfina!"

"Just a moment," says Delfina, maintaining her composure, "I haven't yet expressed my opinion."

"Just say yes, Delfina," the baron insists, "and this will be the most wonderful day of my life."

"But my answer is no."

General consternation, exclamations, and a round of comments: "Well, that's one way to lose a fortune!"; "Now, look at that, a baron's not good enough for her, maybe she wants Prince Charming!"; "Why, that's just bad manners, to say no to such a proper gentleman!"

"Is that a 'no' no, or a 'maybe' no, or a 'wait-and-see' no, or even a 'let's-let-a-little-time-go-by' no?" the baron pushes. "Leave me just a little hope. At least tell me it's a tentative no."

"I wouldn't dream of it. For the moment, the last thing in my mind is marriage."

"And what's the first thing in your mind?" asks Signor Armando.

"The first thing," says Delfina, "is to understand what's behind all this muddle. The baron promised us an explanation."

"You're perfectly right," sighs the baron. (He certainly has a lot of sighing to do today). "I'll tell you everything.

"Last year, in October, I happened to be in Egypt . . ."

Baron Lamberto reveals his secret. He lays out the whole story, including every last detail, while Anselmo vigorously nods in confirmation. Once, in fact, Anselmo breaks in to repeat the exact words of the Arab fakir that they chanced to meet in the shadow of the Sphinx: "Remember that the man whose name is spoken remains alive." Now everything becomes clear in the minds of the twenty-four managing directors. Their suspicions are replaced by swelling emotion. When the baron reaches the point where the bandits cut off first his ear, then his finger, they can no longer contain themselves: they fall to their knees, they kiss his hands, especially the new finger. A couple of the directors even kiss his new ear. When the baron comes to the part where he wakes up in the coffin, Signora Merlo crosses herself and Signora Zanzi, who is an aficionado of the state lottery, murmurs a reference to the Neapolitan book of dreams under her breath: "Dead man talking, that's number 47."

Tears run down Anselmo's cheeks, and he drops his umbrella two or three times. The bank directors bend over and pick it up for him, just to stand out from the crowd.

"Well, that's the whole story," says the baron. "And now, what would you say to drinking a toast to the health of everyone here?"

"Speaking of health," says Delfina, "if I understand what you've just told us, it was us who restored your health."

"That's quite true."

"And we're not even doctors," Delfina goes on. "We're better than wizards. We kept this important personage alive with our voices. With our work. Without even understanding the meaning of what we were doing. For weeks, for months, up in the attic repeating your name like so many parrots on perches, without knowing why. By the way, wouldn't a phonograph record or a tape recording have produced the same effect?"

"No, Signorina," Anselmo explains. "We experimented, but it didn't work."

"It needed the human touch," says Delfina. "You couldn't do it without our lungs. For months we held Baron Lamberto's life in our hands without realizing it, without even suspecting it."

"That's right," Signor Armando exclaims in surprise, "we could have even asked for a raise."

"That's not all," Signor Giacomini realizes in astonishment, "we could have asked for a million dollars. Lord Lamberto, would you have given us a million dollars if we'd asked for it?"

"Why certainly," the baron admits. "Even two million."

"But in that case," Signor Giacomini stammers in amazement, "in that case, in a certain sense, we've been . . . swindled!"

"Swindled my eye!" the director of the Singapore bank explodes. "You were paid very well for your time. I never heard such nonsense!"

"Labor always makes outrageous demands," the director of the Zurich bank comments.

"But now you won't need us anymore," says Delfina.

"Why, that's the furthest thing from my mind," the baron hastens to correct her. "I'll need you as much as before, and price is no object."

"No, Lord Lamberto," one of the secretaries shouts from the bottom of the staircase.

"Not true!"

"What! Who is that and how dare he! Remember your station, sir! Don't say another word."

It seems as if the twenty-four managing directors all want to jump on the poor little secretary at once, to crush him with their executive mass.

"Quiet, quiet," says the baron, intrigued. "Let him talk. . . . Come upstairs, you, speak freely."

"Your Lordship," says the secretary, deeply moved. "You no longer need anyone's help. It's been hours since anyone said your name and yet, as far as I can see, you're alive, you don't seem to be suffering from any physical problems, and you don't show the slightest sign of aging."

"It's true," Anselmo exclaims. "It's quite true, Lord Lamberto!"

"It's true, it's true," cry the twenty-four bank directors, in transports of excitement.

Delfina and her friends look at one another. The baron looks at Delfina. It appears that the story is coming to a decisive turning point.

"Anselmo," says the baron, "let's check."

Anselmo pulls his little notebook out of his pocket and starts checking the twenty-four maladies, of the skeletal structure, of the muscular apparatus, of the circulatory and nervous systems, and so on. Everything is in tiptop shape. There isn't a single cell causing trouble. The circulation of reticulocytes is *increasing.*

"Interesting," murmurs the baron, "interesting. I feel the way I do on my best days. Why would that be?"

"Lord Lamberto," says the little secretary, determined to seize a career opportunity, "there is no mistaking the reason why. You've been reborn, Your Lordship! Your previous life, the life that hung from the thread of the voices of these . . . these six . . . these ladies and gentlemen, is over. Out there, on the lake, a second life began for you. You no longer need anyone! No one at all!"

"Interesting," the baron repeats, "that must be what happened. I really do feel as if I've been reborn. You know, I'm tempted to take a new name, and forget my old one. What would you say to Osvaldo?"

"If I may venture to make a suggestion, what about Renato?" the little secretary said.

"Why Renato?"

"Because it means born twice. And then . . . there's the fact that . . . if you please, my name is Renato, too."

"Very good," the baron says. "Intelligent young man. Anselmo, take note of his surname and address. He deserves a promotion. Very good, it strikes me that at this point we can adjourn the assembly."

"What about us?" asks Signora Merlo.

"Are we fired?" asks Signor Armando.

"Will we at least get severance pay?" asks Signor Bergamini.

The twenty-four managing directors all object in chorus: "Now they want severance pay? What is the world coming to?"

But Baron Lamberto-Renato smiles. A strange smile, though. It looks as if he's planning to play a trick on someone. More of a prank, really.

"Why not?" he says after smiling for a hundred or so seconds. "Severance pay is in order. Anselmo, prepare for each of these three lovely ladies and three courteous gentlemen . . . a little bag of chamomile tea. Choose a particularly fine vintage. I would recommend ... a Tibet 1975."

"Bravo!" roar the managing directors and their personal secretaries.

"Bravissimo!" cries the little secretary Renato, determined to strike while the iron is still hot.

Delfina and her friends sit silent and pensive. And baffled. And indignant. Five pairs of eyes focus on Delfina. Perhaps she has an apt retort. You can tell that she's thinking of one by the way she furrows her brow, from the way she's tapping her knee with her middle finger.

Baron Lamberto is looking at Delfina curiously, too. For a while she sits there, staring into the middle distance, looking at who knows what—perhaps a ceiling beam or a pane of window glass, through which it is possible to see a white cloud sailing majestically past.

"All right," she says, at last, to the surprise of one and all. "We gladly accept the baron's generous gift. His chamomiles are sweet-smelling as the roses of Bulgaria. But we certainly don't want to let him outdo us in generosity, do we? It strikes me that there is a gift that we can offer him in return ..."

"Quite right," approves the director of the Singapore bank. "Pool your savings and give Baron Lamberto a commemorative object, something made of silver or gold."

"Perhaps a tea set," another director suggests.

"A cuckoo clock."

"A keyring shaped like the island of San Giulio."

"Silence, all of you," the baron orders "Let's hear what Delfina has to say."

"Thank you, Lord Lamberto," says Delfina with a slight bow. "I would suggest that my five coworkers and I give the baron, free of charge, and for the very last time, a demonstration of our bravura. After all, in all these months, he's never seen us speak his name. Are you ready?"

And without so much as a glance at her uncomfortable colleagues, Delfina begins: "Lamberto, Lamberto, Lamberto."

Then Signor Armando works up the courage and opens his mouth: "Lamberto, Lamberto, Lamberto."

One by one, the others join the chorus: "Lamberto, Lamberto, Lamberto."

"Fine voices, excellent pronunciation," the butler Anselmo thinks to himself with satisfaction: after all, when this all started, it was he who selected the six speakers out of the hundreds of candidates.

The baron listens with a faint smile poised like a

wasp at the corner of his mouth. Then the smile flies away. Replacing it is a look of astonishment, covering his entire face. The faces of the twenty-four bank directors, too, have shifted from expressions of mere interest and curiosity to open-mouthed incredulity.

Delfina quickens the pace, beating time on one knee with her hand and using gestures and glances to urge her colleagues to go faster and faster.

"Lamberto Lamberto Lamberto."

With the months of training they've had, they easily accelerate from sixty beats a minute to eighty, a hundred, a hundred twenty ... At two hundred beats a minute they resemble six raving demons, battling one another with tongue-twisters for ammunition.

"Lambertolambertolambertolam."

Before the increasingly incredulous eyes of all those present, Baron Lamberto-Renato begins growing younger and younger, rejuvenating visibly and quickly. Now anyone would take him for a twenty-five year old. He's a young man who might be competing in collegiate field and track, a promising actor ready to take the stage and play the role of someone's first sweetheart. His age drops from college degree to high school diploma. And it continues to plummet, as Delfina and her colleagues continue spitting out his name at machine-gun speed:

"Lambertolambertolambertolamberto."

When the baron is just seventeen and his physique is so slender that all his clothing hangs loosely from his frame, he starts to grow shorter too, running backward through his growth years.

"Stop! Stop!" the butler Anselmo shouts in terror.

The twenty-four managing directors stand open-mouthed, incapable of finding words to utter.

Lamberto looks like a little boy dressing up in his father's clothing: his trousers are much longer than his legs, any signs of whiskers have vanished from his face. Now he might be fifteen or so . . .

"Lambertolambertolambertolamber."

"Stop, have mercy!"

Lamberto has a startled expression on his face, he can't really grasp what's happening to him . . . He tugs at the sleeves of his jacket to free his hands. He runs his hand across his face . . .

At this point, he might be about thirteen . . .

And now Delfina stops saying his name and motions to the others to stop as well. Complete silence falls, and Anselmo is seen hightailing it out of the room, but he is back almost immediately, carrying a lovely outfit with short pants. "Master Lamberto, would you care to change into this? It was a gift given to you in nineteen . . .

make that 1896 . . . It's not the latest fashion, but it's just adorable. Come, young master, step this way . . ."

As Anselmo leads Lamberto into an adjoining room to change into something more youthful, sobbing can be heard . . . It's the secretary named Renato crying bitterly.

"I thought," he tells Delfina between sobs, "that you no longer had any power over the life of His Lordship. Alas, it's the end of my career!"

"Now, now," Delfina consoles him, "don't take it so hard, you're still young, tomorrow is another day, etc. etc."

"At least tell me what I got so wrong."

"This is where you went astray," Delfina explains to him patiently. "You developed a theory but you didn't bother to verify it."

"But isn't it true that the baron was feeling well even though no one was pronouncing his name?"

"Perhaps the effect of the funeral was still persisting, with all those people saying his name for free. In any case, I decided to run an experiment. And while I was at it, I also wanted to see what would happen if I introduced the variable of speed. Is that all perfectly clear and distinct?"

"I'll say," Renato sighs. "You certainly have an experimental mindset. Would you marry me?"

"Of course not."

"Why."

"Because I won't."

"Ah, now I see."

But now Lamberto reappears, with Anselmo leading him by the hand, and with the appearance of a bewildered and helpless young boy. He looks around, uncertain what to do next. He looks at the people in the room as if he'd never seen them before. He sees Delfina and a shy smile appears on his little-boy face.

"Delfina," he says, "would you like to become my mommy?"

"That takes the cake," Delfina replies. "First you ask me to be your wife, now you want me to become your mother. Do you always have to reach for me to stand on your own two feet?"

Lamberto looks as if he's about to burst into tears. At that very moment, the managing director of the Shanghai bank, who has been busily consulting with his colleagues, clears his throat and says: "Lord Lamberto ... or rather ... that is ... Master Lamberto ... the situation appears to have changed radically. You are no longer old enough to be the chairman of twenty-four banks in Italy, Switzerland, Hong Kong, Singapore, and elsewhere ... We must appoint a guardian for you, because you're a minor. In the meanwhile . . . we've had an idea. With your attractive youthful face, you seem perfectly suited to win over the hearts of the television audience. We'll make a television commercial for the Lamberto Banks in which you . . . let's see . . . in which you pull the door of the vault shut behind you as you smile and say: 'I'm as safe in here as in my cradle.' What do you think of the idea?"

Lamberto turns to Anselmo, then to Delfina, in search of advice. But Delfina doesn't say a thing. It's up to him this time. He clenches his teeth and his fists. He thinks it over for a long while and then, at last, gets to his feet and says in a firm voice: "Not on your life! My guardian will be Anselmo, who's used to obeying orders from me, not one of you, you old bank guards, you old stuffed owls! As for me, I want to study, I want to . . ."

His face lights up. At last, a broad, happy smile appears on Lamberto's face. He even starts dancing a little jig around the room.

"I want to become an artist in an equestrian circus. That's always been my dream and this time I have a whole lifetime ahead of me to achieve it."

"Bravo!" shouts Signora Zanzi, more deeply moved than ever.

"The idea is absurd, improbable, and even slightly

obscene," declares the director of the Singapore bank.

"You are obscene, absurd, and even slightly obnoxious," Lamberto answers him.

"Bravo!" shouts Signora Merlo.

The bank directors all huddle together and talk. Delfina and the others cluster together and talk. Even Anselmo talks and talks, while Lamberto continues to dance, caper, and stick out his tongue at the gentleman from Singapore.

"I'm going to be a trapeze artist, an acrobat, a juggler, a tightrope dancer, a lion tamer, an elephant trainer, a clown, a trumpeter, and a drummer, and I'll train seals, dogs, fleas, and dromedaries . . ."

He'll do this. He'll do that. What will he do? No one can say yet. But now Delfina is very happy with the gift she dreamed up for him.

Just then, Signor Giacomini—who's grown tired of standing around doing nothing and so has cast his fishing line out the window—reels in a two-pound fish.

"Whoever said that this is a dead lake?" shouts Signor Giacomini excitedly. "Anselmo, grease the pan, we've got fish to fry. And anyone who wants to say anything bad about Lake Orta will have me to answer to."

CHAPTER 13
EPILOGUE

FAIRY TALES USUALLY BEGIN WITH A BOY, a young man, or a girl who experiences a series of adventures and then becomes a prince or a princess, gets married, and then hosts a grand banquet. This fairy tale, on the other hand, begins with a ninety-four-year-old man who, after a number of adventures, becomes a thirteen-year-old boy. Is this an insult to the reader? No, because there's a perfectly good explanation.

Lake Orta, where the island of San Giulio and Baron Lamberto is located, is unlike any of the other lakes in Piedmont and Lombardy, in northern Italy. It's a lake that marches to a different drummer. A freethinker that, instead of sending its water south, the way Lake Maggiore, Lake Como, and Lake Garda do in a proper, disciplined manner, sends its water north, as if to empty into Mount Rosa, instead of the Adriatic Sea.

If you go to Omegna and stand in the Piazza del Municipio, you'll see a river flowing out of Lake Orta that runs due north toward the Alps. It's not a big river, but it's not a little brooklet either. It's called the Nigoglia, and unlike most Italian rivers, it takes a feminine article: La Nigoglia.

The people of Omegna are very proud of this rebellious river, and they've fished up a motto for themselves that says, in dialect:

La Nigoja la va in su
e la legg la fouma nu.

Which means:

La Nigoglia runs uphill
and we make our own laws.

It strikes me as a very nice motto. Always think with your own mind. Of course, in the end, the sea gets its due: in fact, the waters of the Nigoglia, after running northward for a short distance, pour into the Strona, the Strona runs to the Toce, and then into Lake Maggiore, and after that, via the rivers Ticino and Po, those waters pour into the Adriatic Sea. Order is restored. But Lake Orta is still proud of itself for what it's done. Is that a sufficient explanation for a fairy tale that obeys only its own rules? We hope it is.

We should add only that the twenty-four managing directors of the Lamberto Banks, once they returned to their home offices, hastened to hire people, men and women, and pay them to take shifts repeating their highly revered names, day and night. They hoped that this would allow them to recover from their illnesses and turn back time's clock. In vain. Those who had rheumatism were obliged to keep their rheumatism. Those who were bald saw not a hair sprouting from their scalps, neither blond nor brunette. Those who had turned sixty-five did not recover a single minute of their youth. Certain things happen only once. And to tell the truth, certain things can happen only in fairy tales.

Not everyone will be satisfied with the way this story ended. Among other things, no one knows exactly what becomes of Lamberto and what he does when he grows up. There is, however, no remedy for that. Readers who are dissatisfied with the ending are free to change it to suit themselves, adding a chapter or two to this book. Or even thirteen. Never allow yourself to be frightened by the words:

THE END.

LAMBERTO LAMBERTO LAMBERTO LAM
AMBERTO LAMBERTO LAMBERTO LAMBER
RTO LAMBERTO LAMBERTO LAMBERTO L
LAMBERTO LAMBERTO LAMBERTO LAMBI
RTO LAMBERTO LAMBERTO LAMBERTO L
AMBERTO LAMBERTO LAMBERTO LAMB
BERTO LAMBERTO LAMBERTO LAMBERTO L
TO LAMBERTO LAMBERTO LAMBERTO LAMB
ERTO LAMBERTO LAMBERTO LAMBERTO
LAMBERTO LAMBERTO LAMBERTO LA
RTO LAMBERTO LAMBERTO LAMBERTO
AMBERTO LAMBERTO LAMBERTO LAMB
MBERTO LAMBERTO LAMBERTO LAMBE
TO LAMBERTO LAMBERTO LAMB
TO LAMBERTO LAMBERTO LAMBERTO LAM
RTO LAMBERTO LAMBERTO LAMBE
MBERTO LAMBERTO LAMBERTO LAM
ERTO LAMBERTO LAMBERTO LAMBERTO
LAMBERTO LAMBERTO LAMBERTO LA
ETO LAMBERTO LAMBERTO LAMBERTO LAMBER
TO LAMBERTO LAMBERTO LAMBER
MBERTO LAMBERTO LAMBERTO LAMBERTO
ERTO LAMBERTO LAMBERTO LAMBERTO L
ERTO LAMBERTO LAMBERTO LAMBERTO LAMBERTO
ERTO LAMBERTO LAMBERTO LAMBERTO L
RTO LAMBERTO LAMBERTO LAM
AMBERTO LAMBERTO LAMBERTO LAM
BERTO LAMBERTO LAMBERTO LAMBERT.
LAMBERTO LAMBERT. LAMBERTO
ERTO LAMBERTO LAMBERT
RTO LAMBERTO LAMBERTO LAMBERTO L
TO LAMBERTO LAMBERTO LAMBER
ERTO LAMBERTO LAMBERTO LAMBERTO LAM
ERTO LAMBERT. LAMBERTO LAMBER
O LAMBERTO LAMBERTO LAMBERTO LAM